He survived by

She's about to make him melt.

SWEET

It's 2004, and Daisy Rivera knows two things: she's going to end up disappointing her parents' fondest hopes and dreams in roughly six months, and somehow she's going to figure out how to kiss Spider, the mysterious tattoo artist two shops down from her grandmother's café.

Spider Villalobos knows one thing: if he gives in to temptation and makes a move on Daisy, his fresh start is *over*.

Their shops may be neighbors in Metlin, but their lives are worlds apart.

SWEET is a brand-new novella in the Love Stories on 7th and Main series by *USA Today* best-selling author, Elizabeth Hunter.

PRAISE FOR ELIZABETH HUNTER

If you're a fan of contemporary romance and haven't tried the 7th and Main series by Elizabeth Hunter yet, then you have an awesome, satisfying reading experience ahead of you.

KYLIE SCOTT, NYT BESTSELLING AUTHOR

This is everything I could have asked for and then some. I have never read a book more aptly named!

THIS LITERARY LIFE

"Sweet" is definitely sweet *and* spicy, and the perfect novella to curl up with this holiday season!

KATHRYN, GOODREADS REVIEWER

Book lovers will enjoy Emmie's literary swoons, while those who thrill to bad boys will enjoy Ox's blunt talk and big heart.

ADRIAN LIANG, AMAZON BOOK REVIEW

This is simply pure fun. It's what you want a book to deliver. You will walk away with a whole new "book family" not just book boyfriend.

This is everything that made me fall in love with romance.

Heartwarming, sexy, swoony and so adorable! I adored Elizabeth Hunter's first Love Stories on 7th and Main Series with Emmie and Ox, and this one with Tayla and Jeremy didn't disappoint.

SWEET: A NOVELLA

A LOVE STORY ON 7TH AND MAIN

ELIZABETH HUNTER

CHAPTER 1

DAISY SAW him through the dusty window of Metlin Books as soon as she turned the corner. She froze for a second, trying to figure out what Spider Villalobos was doing there; then she remembered that the tattoo artist was an old friend of Betsy Elliot, the owner of Metlin Books.

Shit! This was not part of her plan. This was one hundred percent not at all in the plan.

Daisy was usually the one who dropped off the café's rent check at the bookstore, but Spider had never been behind the counter before. It was usually just Betsy or sometimes her granddaughter Emmie, a chatty fourteen-year-old with a quietly wicked sense of humor.

Spider was... Spider. Medium height and build with a closely cropped head of nearly black hair, dark eyes, and a jaw as sharp as a knife. He had high, arched cheekbones, and black-and-grey tattoos spread from his neck, disappeared into his shirt, and reappeared down both arms to the wrist. He even had tattoos on the back of his hands and a few on his knuckles.

Oh my God, oh my God, oh my God.

This could not be happening. Daisy looked okay that afternoon, but she hadn't planned on seeing *Spider*. She was wearing the jeans she'd worn for gardening the weekend before and a T-shirt she'd planned on changing when she got to the café.

She was not supposed to be seeing Spider.

The only direct interaction Daisy had with Spider was when he stopped by her family's bakery, Café Maya, to grab his regular coffee—black, three sugars—before he headed over to Misspent Youth, the tattoo shop across from the bookshop.

Those short interactions had a set order. He offered her a muttered "What's up?" She smiled and poured his coffee into a mug he brought from home that was meticulously washed. He paid in cash. She said, "Thanks for coming to Café Maya; have a good morning."

And that was that.

She had to go into the bookshop. Lingering outside the plate glass windows wasn't an option. Turning around wasn't either; she was pretty sure he'd already seen her.

Daisy pushed open the door to the bookshop, the jingle of the bell over the door barely audible over her pounding heart. Spider glanced up, then looked intently at something on the counter. Then he looked up again as she approached the counter and didn't take his eyes off her for a second.

He lifted his chin in a small nod. "What's up?"

Daisy swallowed hard. "Uh…" Oh my God, she was an idiot. Who started talking to someone as hot as Spider with an uh? "I just… I have the rent check for Betsy." She pulled the envelope from her back pocket. "For the café. It's the first."

"Okay." He stared at her but didn't elaborate.

Daisy frowned a little. "Is she here?"

"Appointment."

Apparently her object of fascination for eight months only spoke in single words.

"Okay…" Daisy wasn't sure what to say. Would Betsy want her to leave the check with Spider? She obviously trusted him to watch the shop, so dropping off a check—

"Spider!" There was a thundering set of footsteps from the hallway to the left of the counter, and a young teenager with reddish-brown hair poked her head in the doorway. "Oh hey, Daisy. Are you looking for a book? I can help you find one."

It was Emmie, Betsy's granddaughter. Daisy immediately smiled; Emmie was five years younger than her, but she always made Daisy laugh.

"Hey, Em. I wish I was here to get a new read, but I'm just dropping off the rent check for your grandma."

"Oh." Emmie stalked forward with her hand out. "I can take it. I know where she puts them in her office."

"Cool." Daisy glanced at Spider for a second before she handed over the envelope. "Thanks."

"No problem." Emmie grabbed the check and walked behind the counter, leaning into Spider a little bit. She smiled a little. "What were you and Spider talking about?"

Daisy blinked. "I... We weren't actually—"

"Mimi, mind your business," Spider said quietly. "Homework, remember?"

So he didn't only speak in single words. That was a relief.

"Ugh." Emmie rolled her eyes to the heavens. "It's a report on the Roman Empire; like... the most boring thing ever."

"Latin is a kick-ass language, and the Romans did shit in Europe that's still relevant today." He nudged her with his elbow. "Study."

Daisy watched the short interplay between the two— so similar to her conversations with her little brother Kiko—and realized that Spider treated Emmie like a little sister. He had a nickname for her and reminded her about her homework.

Which was completely unfair because it only made him hotter.

"Okay." Daisy backed toward the door. "I'm going to just head back to the café." She offered a small wave. "See you."

"Thanks." He glanced at Emmie. "For the rent. I'll tell Betsy you dropped it off."

It was the longest thing he'd said to her since she'd first noticed him eight months before. "Thanks for coming to Café— Uh, I mean…" *Oh God, kill me now.*

The corner of Spider's mouth turned up; he knew he made her nervous.

"Anyway, thanks!" Her voice squeaked. "For telling Betsy." She waved again. "Bye, Emmie. Bye…" Had they been introduced? He'd never told her his name; she'd just asked around. "Have a good morning." It was afternoon. "Good afternoon. Have a good…" She spun around and headed for escape. "Bye."

Emmie yelled behind her. "Come back when you want a book!"

Daisy felt his eyes on her back as she walked to the door—her face had to be on literal fire—but as soon as she pushed the handle and the fresh air hit her face, she realized she'd exited in the wrong place. She'd come in through the door on 7th Avenue, but the café was on Main Street and that's the direction she was supposed to go because she needed to head to work.

There is no going back.

Forget turning around—she was just going to walk all the way around the block the other way because there was no way on God's green earth she was going to walk past Metlin Books on the corner again.

Nope.

In fact, eight months of careful planning, preparation, and outfits that showed exactly the right amount of cleavage had just flown out the door. She was probably going to need to move. Maybe her parents had the right idea after all. Going to a university six hours away from home was an excellent idea, and it would save her from ever seeing Spider again.

Ever.

Again.

———

DAISY PUSHED OPEN THE GARDEN GATE AT HER parent's house on Church Street and was immediately assaulted by the cacophony of cousins.

"Daisy!"

"Hey, Didi."

"Rudy, pass the friggin' baaaaall. Come ooooon."

One of her youngest cousins scampered up to poke at the distinctive pink box she was carrying. "You brought pie!"

Daisy looked down at Amelia and cocked her hip, balancing the pie while she took off her sunglasses. "Want to guess what kind?"

"Ummm." The ten-year-old girl put her nose to the box and inhaled loudly.

"Amelia!" Daisy burst out laughing.

"Lemon!" The little girl ran off without a backward glance, bold as a blue jay and just as loud.

I used to be that way.

She liked to think she still was on the inside, but at nineteen, Daisy couldn't escape the fact that she was one of the oldest of her cousins, her great-aunt's favorite, and the designated "success in the making" for her family. The pressure was starting to get to her.

Daisy waved at various cousins, aunts, and uncles as she headed toward the detached garage next to the kitchen. It was an old house built in the 1920s that her Mexican grandparents had bought as a wreck, then fixed up over the years as they built a life in Central California.

When Maya had passed away in her fifties, her children might have been grown, but they still needed a mother. Which was why, with not a second thought, Daisy's great-aunt, Tia Imelda, had moved from Mexico to help Daisy's parents with the house and the bakery.

Now the built-in woodwork shone with love and lemon oil, and the house that Maya and Enrique Rivera had built contained their two children, a son- and daughter-in-law, six grandchildren, and half of Daisy's mother's family who had all grown up in the house next door.

Along with at least three Chihuahuas at any given time.

The Riveras and the Oroscos had run in and out of the others' houses as if they were their own. Luckily, Daisy's parents, Roberto and Alicia, had decided to get married and formalize the family connection.

They were restauranteurs and contractors, farmers, warehouse managers, and salon owners. Daisy came from people who knew how to work hard and take care of their family no matter what.

But she would be the first one to attend a university. The first one of her cousins, ranked second in her graduating high school class, the pride of the Riveras and Oroscos.

A soccer ball went flying past her, chased by two of her boy cousins and one of Imelda's Chihuahuas named Ronaldinho, who was unsuccessfully trying to live up to his name.

"If you trip me with that soccer ball while I'm carrying pie" —Daisy snapped at the older one— "I will shave your head, I swear it."

The smaller one's eyes went wide, but his older brother laughed. "Your fault for wearing those shoes."

He ducked away before she could throw one at him.

She set the lemon meringue pie in the garage refrigerator and followed the sound of chatter toward the kitchen.

Daisy was reminded *daily* how proud everyone was. Her mother and father. Her aunts and uncles. Her great-aunt and even her grandparents who'd passed before she was born. She knew because her aunt told her every morning after mass.

"Hey, Mom." She glanced at the flurry of activity as she walked to the sink to wash her hands. "I brought a pie; it's in the fridge. Can I do anything?"

Her mother was stirring the pot of beans on the stovetop while Tia Imelda sat at the kitchen table, scraping the spines off nopales so they could be sliced and put on the grill next to the carne asada that she'd smelled cooking outside.

"Hey, mija." Her mom's sister Dolores patted the chair between her and Imelda. "Get these chiles ready for the salsa."

The smoky scent of charred pepper skin met Daisy's nose as she sat and started peeling the cracked blackened skin from the roasted chiles. She'd only been working for a few minutes when the questions started.

"So what did the financial aid office at UC Davis say?"

"Have you already gotten your transfer application in? Which schools did you apply for?"

"What options are there for student housing? Like, do you still live in dorms or something? Even when you're twenty? How expensive is that?"

After high school, Daisy had taken the frugal, practical route of attending the local community college for her general education. Her business-minded parents could appreciate that since they avoided debt like other people avoided lava or undercooked chicken.

But with her general education on track to finish the following spring, she needed to fill out her applications to transfer to a larger university. She had incredible grades. Great transcripts and extracurricular activities. No matter where she applied, her guidance counselor was confident she would get in.

The only problem? She didn't want to go.

Daisy nodded and made polite and vague answers to all her aunts' and cousins' questions, but her heart wasn't in it.

She didn't know how to explain it to them! Her brother Kiko had always been the quiet, methodical type, doing well in school but working at their father's construction company every weekend with every expectation that Rivera General Contractors would eventually turn into Rivera and Son's General Contracting.

And Daisy would go to university and become... what?

"Have you thought about psychology, mija?" her mother asked. "You'd be so good at that. You could work with kids, really make a difference that way."

Daisy's mother had the biggest heart on the planet, so she'd heard that suggestion before.

"What about, like... history or archaeology or something like that?" Her cousin Roni's eyes lit up. "You could travel and stuff. Find treasures like Indiana Jones."

Her cousin Olivia turned and grinned at her. "Indiana Rivera!"

"I don't think real archaeologists have lives like in the movies." Daisy had to laugh. And cry. On the inside where nooooo one could see it. "I was thinking about botany?" Daisy shrugged. "I don't know. I like plants."

The problem with all her family's suggestions was none of them were staying home and taking over the café downtown, which was what she really wanted to do. Olivia and Roni were starting their own salon once Roni graduated. Her mother kept making noises about wanting to retire. Imelda hardly moved from the register most days. Why wasn't the café good enough for Daisy?

"Being a great gardener does not mean you should study plants at a university," her tia Angie said. "What would you do with a botany degree? Is that for research or something?"

Tia Imelda reached over and patted Daisy's hand. "My niece already *is* a great gardener. You should be teaching them, not the other way."

"Thanks, Tia." She looked up. "I'm planning on taking some business classes in the spring. Maybe I'll like those."

"Oooh!" Roni's eyes lit up again. "Can you imagine Daisy in, like, a superhot business suit? You'd look so bomb. You could, like, trade stocks and stuff on Wall Street and be so fu—"

A collective gasp cut her off. "Veronica Cristina Jimenez Orosco!"

"Freaking rich!" Roni's face was red. "That's all I was going to say, that Daisy could trade stocks and be so *freaking* rich. That's all."

Or I could run a café on Main Street.

Her mother hit the back of her cousin's head. "And why would she learn about business from some professors and not her aunties or her dad? You think those professors have ever done payroll or negotiated a contract? No, Daisy is going to study something *important*." Her mom motioned to Roni. "And you're next, so you better not be late with your Spanish homework again. Your mom told me you've been slacking off."

"Why do I have to freaking take Spanish when I speak it, Tia? It's sooooo stupid."

"So you should be getting an A+ and not a C! What is that?" The volume of the debate in the kitchen slowly rose higher and higher as Daisy managed to shrink into the background, nearly finished peeling the charred chiles.

She pursed her lips, relieved that the attention of the room was on her high school cousins and not on her.

Daisy felt a nudge on her toe, and she looked up to see Imelda looking at her.

Her aunt smiled, her face creasing into soft, comforting seams. "They'll figure it out," she said softly.

"Figure what out?"

"You know." Imelda winked and went back to scraping the sharp needles off the cactus leaves. "Remember, *el corazón es lo que mueve el mundo*."

Daisy smiled. "I don't think my heart is moving Mom and Dad's plans, much less the world, Tia."

"That's because you haven't found the thing that anchors it yet." Imelda's knife scraped along the cactus leaf, carefully shearing off the prickly spines. "But you will."

CHAPTER 2

SPIDER'S ALARM went off at eight thirty every morning no matter how late he'd worked the night before. He was an early riser by habit, but that didn't line up with tattoo-shop hours. Most days he worked until midnight, often until one or two in the morning if the piece was complicated or a last-minute walk-in had cash.

He was still the new guy; he didn't get to pick his hours.

Rubbing his eyes, Spider tried to figure out why he was so sleepy. He'd gotten over six hours of sleep the night before—that should have been more than enough.

He closed his eyes and immediately remembered.

A cloud of curly brown hair, hazel-brown eyes, bright red lipstick leaving trails of red smudges over his chest. Her sweet pink tongue peeking out from between her lips as she—

Fuuuuuck him. He rubbed his eyes. He was not

allowed to have sex dreams about sweet, innocent Daisy Rivera, pride of Metlin and his own personal fantasy wrapped up in a red polka-dot dress.

Spider rolled out of bed and immediately went to splash water on his face. He pulled on a pair of grey sweats, ignoring the semi in his boxer briefs. He grabbed the pull-up bar from under his bed and hung it over the closet door in the small studio apartment over his boss's garage.

There was an old radio sitting in the windowsill that had been there when he moved in. He flipped it on and was immediately greeted by the sounds of the morning show on the oldies station.

"—starting the morning out with 98.9, the best of claaaaassic rock and doo-wop filling your morning drive. Let's start the morning with that eternal question: Why do those fools fall in love, Harry?"

"I don't know, JJ, but they're driving their parents craaaaazy."

The morning-show hosts bantered back and forth as a familiar song filled the empty apartment, taking Spider back to the happiest memories he had of his childhood, sitting in the corner of the automotive-upholstery shop where his dad worked, listening to the radio and drawing in his sketch pad.

He counted out fifty pull-ups, five sets of ten, alternating with fifty push-ups, also in sets of ten. Then he grabbed the exercise bands he'd bought at the swap meet and worked on leg presses and sit-ups.

Spider didn't like spending money on gyms, and he didn't like showing his skin to anyone who might know what his ink meant. His arms weren't too bad, but his chest revealed the violence of his teenage years. Plus a lot of it was just jacked-up work from shitty artists who didn't know what they were doing.

Part of his pay at Misspent Youth was Ruby, his boss's wife, doing cover work for some of the worst shit. He wasn't enough of an idiot to tattoo himself, but he trusted Ruby.

He exercised for nearly an hour; then he took a shower and did not think about Daisy Rivera. Then he heated up a packet of plain oatmeal and didn't think about the strawberry pie he'd seen at the café two days before.

I wish I was here to get a new read...

She'd said that in the bookshop the day before. She liked to read, which made sense because she was a smart girl. Yeah, that fit. Everyone talked about how well she did in school, how she'd be heading off to some fancy university soon.

Spider leaned against the small counter in the corner of the apartment and methodically finished off his oatmeal. He pictured Daisy in a pair of jeans like she'd been wearing the day before, a backpack on her shoulder, hanging with the smart people at a college somewhere. In his imagination, she was wearing glasses, which was stupid because she didn't need them, but whatever. They looked cute on her.

Everything looked fucking cute on her.

He rinsed out his bowl, dried it, and set it back on the small shelf where he kept the few pieces of kitchen gear he owned. Most of them he'd gotten from Betsy or picked up at the swap meet, but they worked and if anyone stole them, he wouldn't be mad.

After Spider cleaned the kitchen, he made his bed and tossed his clothes and his towel in the laundry basket in the corner. He had two more days before he needed to do laundry, so he made a mental note to get quarters at the bank when he deposited his paycheck.

He put on a clean pair of jeans, a crisp white T-shirt, and a clean blue-and-white-plaid flannel he'd ironed the night before. He might be a poor motherfucker with no useful education, but he wasn't a slob. He brushed his teeth and straightened his collar in the small mirror over the sink.

Spider had a paycheck now, a real one. A social security card and something on file with the IRS. He had a license with the state board that said he was legally qualified to do the job he'd been doing since he was fourteen years old.

Those documents were all under his legal name—which no one in LA knew him by—but it was still stressing him out. He'd felt pretty anonymous when he'd been working under the table, but the last time he called south, Chino was still running his old neighborhood, and Chino had a long memory.

Legal documents. Public records. All that felt

dangerous to a homeboy who'd been hiding for five years.

If he needed to pick up and leave Metlin, he could do it within an hour, and everything he valued would fit in the back of his dad's 1970 El Camino, which was the one thing he'd brought from LA and the last piece of his father he owned. He'd sold his mom's jewelry and his dad's watch. He had his grandma's gold medallion necklace with the Virgin on it, his dad's car, and that was it.

Spider grabbed his keys and headed out the door, already thinking about seeing Daisy at Café Maya before he went to work. He wondered what she'd be wearing. Wondered if the red polka-dot shirt would make an appearance again.

Then he mentally kicked his own ass for wondering.

He had a job, his dad's El Camino, and his grandmother's medal. That was all he needed. All he could allow himself to need. Anything past that was way too dangerous.

———

"So glad Daisy was able to drop off the rent check on time." Betsy was mixing a salad with two big forks, and Spider was watching what she put in it this time. The week before, she'd snuck some raisins in the salad, and that was not cool.

He registered what the old lady had said about Daisy. "She not turn the rent check in on time before?"

"Oh no. I don't think any of the Riveras have been late on a bill in their lives." She glanced up at Spider. "Which is admirable, but sometimes even the best of us get behind. It's the hardware store this month."

That didn't surprise Spider. The hardware store was fucking dusty. Every time he walked into that place, he wanted to sneeze. No one went in the hardware store anymore except a few old guys who knew Mr. Vasquez, the owner. There was a dominoes game every Thursday morning out front; otherwise, he never saw traffic.

"It's busy on Saturday, and sometimes on farmers' market nights, but other than that..." Betsy shook her head. "Of course, I'm one to talk."

"People come into the bookshop," Spider said. "I see them all the time."

"Oh, they come in, all right. I have lots of customers." She smiled. "Lots of company. But they tend to buy the used books, and I can't charge much for those."

Spider couldn't say anything, but he made a mental note to buy something from Betsy the next time he got paid. He owed his entire new life to the old lady.

"So they're not paying the rent," he said. "When are you gonna kick them out?"

"Spider!" Betsy looked shocked. "I'm not going to kick them out."

"But the rent is what pays the bills, right?" He frowned. "If they're not paying the rent—"

"They'll catch up when they can." Betsy patted his

shoulder. "I've known Ernie for years. I can't just kick him out. Main Street Hardware is an institution."

Institutions didn't always make money though.

Spider looked down at the pile of broccoli he'd chopped. "Is this enough?"

"That's perfect, honey." Betsy took the cutting board from him and dumped it into a steamer basket on the stove. "The roast will be done in just a few minutes and then we'll eat."

Eating Sunday dinner at Betsy's was the first time Spider had ever really had what he thought of as "white-people food." When he was little, his mom always had something on the stove. Fresh tortillas with butter melting in the middle, breakfast tacos tucked into his dad's lunchbox, burritos in his backpack for lunch. His mom hated when he asked to eat the cafeteria food at school; she said it was garbage food.

After his dad died, his mom didn't have time to cook. She gave him money to buy food, but he spent it on junk. He was pretty sure he ate nothing but tortilla chips his entire eighth grade year.

When he was running with Chino's crew, he ate whatever was at the house, and sometimes that was a home-cooked dinner. Sometimes it almost felt like a family.

Until it didn't.

"Spider, can you put the placemats on the table?"

"Yeah." He walked to the built-in cupboards that covered one wall of the kitchen and grabbed the plastic-covered mats and set them on the table. One for Betsy, one for him, and one for Emmie.

Regular old family dinner, only with soupy beef instead of chile verde and beans.

"Emmie," Betsy called. "Put your book down and come to the table."

Emmie's mom, Yvonne, was touring with her band that weekend and had two gigs in Sacramento. Yvonne was funny, but she reminded Spider of the women who would flit around the edges of Chino's crew, hungry for attention and excitement.

Emmie rounded the corner and hung on the door-jamb of the kitchen. "What are we having?"

"Pot roast." Betsy took the lid off the brown pot thing with the glass lid, and the aroma filled the kitchen. Spider's mouth started to water, but Emmie groaned.

"I thought you were going to make lasagna."

Betsy put the beef roast in a large bowl and rounded up the potatoes in the soup pot, spooning them out of the soup and placing them around the roast. "I didn't have time to make lasagna, honey. If you help out in the shop next week Sunday, maybe we can do it then."

Emmie looked like she was going to protest again, but Spider caught her eye and raised an eyebrow. She shut up.

They'd had a conversation a couple of weeks ago about not complaining when people fed you. No matter what it was, that food had taken time, effort, and money. You should be fucking grateful even if you didn't like it.

Emmie went to the fridge and opened it. "What do you want to drink, Spider?"

"Coke."

"Water for me," Betsy said.

"Can I have a Coke?" Emmie asked.

Betsy sat at the table and let out a tired breath. "Emmie, no. You'll be up all night if you drink caffeine. Have water, milk, or juice."

"Grandma, oh my Go—"

"You know what? I'll have juice." Spider cut off her protest. "I'm not working tonight, so I should cut the caffeine. Try to get to sleep a little earlier, you know?"

Betsy offered him a grateful smile as Emmie filled their juice glasses and she served the roast. "Did you have a busy week?"

"Pretty busy." He waited until everyone had food on their plate before he started to eat. "Rudy hooked me up with a guy who wants a full back piece, so that's pretty cool."

Betsy said, "That sounds complicated. Will it take a long time?"

Spider smiled a little. "Yeah. It'll take a while 'cause he wants it in color. I guess the guy said he'd seen one of my pieces on another guy at his work, so that was pretty cool."

She patted his hand. "That's wonderful; you're going to have your own shop if you keep working so hard."

Betsy was always interested in his job even though she was, like, the last lady in the universe who would ever get a tattoo or even be interested in them. It was a damn miracle she'd given him the time of day when he showed up at her store, looking for work. He could cover his sleeves, but not the ink on his neck. He thought for sure she'd kick him out, and he was ready to run if she picked up the phone and called the cops.

Spider reached for his glass of apple juice and watched Emmie across the table. The little shit looked like she was in the mood to start something, and Spider knew it would be something to do with him. Emmie loved tormenting him.

Of course, he did his share of tormenting her, so it was only fair.

"Daisy was acting superweird when she dropped off the rent check," Emmie said.

Don't you dare. Spider narrowed his eyes and shook his head a little.

Emmie grinned so hard her dimple popped out. "I think she likes Spider."

Betsy's eyebrows went up and her mouth formed a surprised *O*. "Is that so?"

"She's just being friendly." Spider did not need Betsy getting interested in his love life. Or lack of it. "We see each other at the café most days, you know?"

Emmie pressed her lips together, keeping her eyes on him. "I know. She said bye like she was seeing him at the café. It was pretty embarrassing."

Spider glared at her. "People misspeak. It happens."

"Well." Betsy was smiling. "You know I love Daisy

Rivera. She's such a bright girl and an incredibly hard worker. I think the two of you—"

"She's a kid." Spider cut Betsy off even though he could practically hear his mother screaming at him for interrupting an elder. "I mean… she's nice and all, but isn't she going to college next year or something? That's what I heard."

"She was second in her entire senior class," Betsy said. "Can you believe that?"

"Uh-huh." Spider concentrated on eating his roast, glaring at Emmie when Betsy was distracted.

The last thing he needed was Emmie or Betsy playing matchmaker. He had enough stress in his life without thinking about Daisy harboring a crush on him and anyone encouraging her. Emmie was imagining things, and Spider didn't need the trouble.

Because even if she was interested, Spider knew he was the last thing a girl like Daisy Rivera needed.

CHAPTER 3

DAISY STOOD outside the Ice House on the corner of 7th and Main with Roni while Olivia argued with Stan, the guy doing security out front of the bar.

"We'll keep track of Roni, okay?" Olivia was the most reasonable of her cousins. If anyone could talk them into the bar, it was her.

Roni leaned against the painted cinder block and looked down 7th Avenue. "Do you think any of the guys from the tattoo shop are inside?"

Daisy's mind immediately jumped to Spider. "I have no idea. It's not like I come here all the time or something."

"Some of those guys are kinda gross, but a couple of them are way hot." Roni kicked her feet against the wall. "You know the one with the buzz-cut hair?"

Daisy bit her lip, grateful to see Olivia waving them over. "Oh look. Come on."

Stan held up his hand before the girls could enter. "You" —he pointed at Roni— "do not go anywhere with any of these dudes alone. Do you hear me?"

Roni rolled her eyes. "Oh my God, Stan. I'm just here to hang out and have a beer."

"No fucking beer." Stan glared at Olivia. "You told me—"

"She's kidding." Daisy tugged on Roni's arm and stepped on the edge of her shoe. "Kidding. She's just being a brat. We're not drinking; we just want to hang with Olivia."

Stan was still suspicious. "I'm not worried about you, Daisy."

Olivia walked up and put her arm around Roni's shoulders. "We'll keep her in line. And we won't sit at the bar. Promise."

He raised one finger. "No slipups and no problems. You don't get a second chance."

"Okay!" Daisy shuffled Roni into the bar before her little cousin could get another word in. Technically, the Ice House was eighteen and up, but since Roni was close and Stan was best friends with Olivia's older brother, he usually let them in as long as the bar was quiet.

"Don't give Stan a heart attack." Olivia laughed a little. "Roni, I swear you're going to get us all arrested one of these days."

"You'd be so bored without me." She fiddled with one of the gold hoops that danced up the shell of her ear. "So what can I drink?"

"Not beer."

"I don't want to look like a baby or something," Roni hissed. "I promise I won't drink, but—"

"I'll get you a soda with a slice of lime." Olivia pointed to one of the tall tables near the old-fashioned jukebox. "No one will know the difference."

"Just a root beer for me," Daisy said.

"Okay, cool." Olivia put her purse down in the seat and headed toward the bar. "No boys, Roni."

Roni looked around the bar and crinkled her nose. "It's not exactly like there's a ton of options tonight anyway. Why aren't there more cute guys in Metlin?"

"Give it time." Daisy put her purse on the empty seat and leaned her elbows on the table. "Most guys look better when they get older." She glanced at Olivia, who was leaning on the bar and whispering to Nestor, the reason they were there. "What do you think about Nestor?"

"He's okay." Roni shrugged. "I don't like that goatee thing he grew, but his body is nice and—"

"Oh my God, Roni." Daisy laughed. "He's Olivia's boyfriend. I'm not talking about his looks."

Roni blinked. "So what do you—?"

"Like, do you think he's nice? Do you think he's good for her?"

Roni frowned. "How should I know? I mean, who has she been with besides Nestor? Would you want to buy the first car you ever drove?"

Daisy felt her cheeks get hot. "Definitely not."

Her first sexual experience with a boy had been anything but memorable. She'd left with a vague sense of awkward embarrassment and a burning curiosity why the world was so obsessed with all that.

"See? Nestor is, like, the only guy Olivia's ever dated. Boring. I don't want to get married until I'm, like, thirty at least. I don't even want a boyfriend until then."

Daisy raised a skeptical eyebrow. "Oh really?"

"I mean, I'll hook up with a hot guy, but I'm not gonna let him tie me down."

The door swung open and a group of men entered, one of them laughing so loud that the entire bar turned to look.

"Nice." Roni smiled. "Tattoo boys."

Daisy's eyes landed on Spider, who was drifting near the back of the group, his inked skin vivid next to his bright white T-shirt, a worn flannel slung around his waist. It wasn't often that she saw him wearing short sleeves, but the warm fall evening was just barely cooling off.

"I think they hang out here most nights." Daisy knew it. She'd seen them when she worked evening shifts at the café. "It's right across the street."

"That really hot guy in back?" Roni leaned closer as Olivia approached with their drinks. "They call him Spider, and I heard he's from LA and he's in a gang and everything." Roni sat back in her seat, her eyes wide as if she'd just dropped a bomb.

"Don't be dumb." Olivia set their drinks down. "Metlin boys only think they're in gangs."

"I said he was from LA."

Olivia leaned her elbow on the table and dropped her voice. "Keep your voice down, idiot. You think a real gang member is gonna move up to Metlin and start working at Bill and Ruby's tattoo studio? That guy has been in Metlin for years." She jumped onto the tall chair. "He's friends with Betsy Elliot. He just started working at the tattoo place; he used to work at a ranch or something. Nestor says he's cool."

Daisy couldn't take her eyes off him. She kept looking away, but inevitably her eyes would end up back on Spider, who'd taken a seat at a long table in the far corner of the bar. His arms were crossed over his chest, and the dark cross that covered one elbow pointed toward her.

Daisy watched him pick up a beer bottle and pour it into a glass before he lifted the drink to his lips. His throat moved as he swallowed, and the dark flourishes on his neck moved like waves. He set down his drink and his eyes scanned the bar, falling on her before she could look away.

She jerked her gaze away from him but felt as if his eyes were burning her skin. She looked at Olivia, who was talking about something Nestor had told her at the bar.

"Daisy?"

"Hmm?" She looked at Roni.

"Why is the hot tattoo boy staring at you?" Her cousin was smiling like she'd discovered a secret. "Do you know him?"

"No! I don't *know* him. He comes in the café sometimes to get coffee before work." She shook her head. "That's all. He seems nice."

"So what kind of coffee does he get?" Olivia asked.

"Just coffee. Normal coffee."

"That's dumb." Roni snorted. "Ruby keeps a pot of coffee at Misspent all the time. She offered me some when I went in with Ashley Nelson to get her ear pierced."

Olivia's gaze swung to Daisy. "Is that so? Just regular coffee he could get at work but he pays for. At the café." Her cousin leaned forward and tapped her finger on her chin. "Why would he do that, I wonder?"

Daisy felt her cheeks heating up again. "Shut up. He probably just doesn't like how Ruby makes the coffee. Don't make a big thing about—"

"He keeps looking at you," Roni said. "He looks away, nods at his buddies—does the guy ever smile?— then he glances over here again." Roni lifted her hand and waved. "Hi!"

Daisy slapped her leg. "Stop it!"

Olivia hissed. "Roni, don't be a brat."

Roni pouted. "Looks like I scared him away."

Daisy's head popped up. "What?"

"He's walking out. See?"

She saw Spider heading toward the back door; she

looked at the table. No one was bidding him goodbye, which probably meant he was just going outside for a cigarette or something.

"Roni, don't tease her," Olivia said. "She obviously likes the guy."

"I don't like him," Daisy stammered. "Like, *like* him, I mean. I just— He seems like a nice person. He knows Emmie; he's sweet and everything. With her. Emmie. He knows Betsy, remember? I saw him at the bookshop the other day, and he was kind of watching her." Daisy reached for her drink, wishing suddenly that Nestor had ignored her request and given her a real beer. "Stop staring at me."

"Daisy has a cruuuuuush," Olivia whispered, "on the mysterious tattoo artist."

"Get some." Roni did a little dance in her chair and Olivia laughed. "Hey, what do you have to lose? You're heading off to some fancy college next year anyway. You might as well have a little fun before you go."

"Honestly, Daisy, you really do need to fool around with someone besides Johnny Rosa." Olivia leaned closer. "I mean, did the entire experience even pass fifteen min—"

"Oh my God, please shut up and never mention this again ever in my life." Daisy pressed her hands to her face, which felt like it had been baking on the surface of the sun. "I can't believe I even told you it happened."

"I didn't hear about that!" Roni protested.

Olivia said, "Yeah, cause you were, like, fourteen."

"Three years?" Roni was incredulous. "You're twenty. Are you telling me—?"

"I have an idea." Daisy felt desperate. "If I go out and talk to that man, will you two stop talking about my lack of a love life? For, like, the entire night?"

Olivia pressed her lips together and nodded, her eyes laughing.

"Oh man," Roni whined. "That means if you go talk to him, we can't ask you about it when you come back?"

Daisy nodded. "Correct."

Roni looked at Olivia. "I can't promise that; I might die."

"Do it!" Olivia slapped Roni's arm. "It's only one night."

Roni looked back at Daisy and narrowed her eyes. "You're evil."

"Agree or not?"

"How do we know you actually talked to him?"

Olivia jumped in. "You have to get his phone number!"

Fuck.

"Fine." She could always write a random phone number on a napkin and pretend it was Spider's. "I'll get his phone number."

Now Roni was looking at her with new respect. "I like this Daisy. We should take her out more often."

"Oh, shut up." Daisy slid off the stool and grabbed her purse before she headed toward the door where Spider had disappeared without a backward glance.

Shit. Shit shit shit.

She was heading out to the back of the Ice House, and she had to talk to Spider.

Kill me now.

———

SHE PUSHED THE DOOR OPEN AND FELT momentarily lost by the sudden shift from light to dark.

The backyard of the Ice House was mostly a collection of old wooden picnic tables scarred from cigarettes and matches. There was a horseshoe pit in the far corner and a line of half-burned-out Christmas lights to illuminate the darkness.

Most of the tables were occupied with small groups of people sharing cigarettes and speaking closely. There were a few meshed shadows of couples making out.

"You don't look like a smoker."

Daisy spun and saw Spider leaning against the fence in the corner, the tip of his cigarette glowing in the shadows.

"I don't smoke... much." She blinked hard and drifted toward him. "I just needed some air. My cousins are... Yeah."

"Huh." He nodded.

Holy shit, she was having an actual conversation with Spider. Kind of. And it wasn't about his coffee.

"Is that who you're with?" He took another draw on

his cigarette. "I didn't know Nestor's girl was your cousin."

"Yeah." She nodded and walked toward him, shoving her hands in her jacket pockets to hide the shaking. "She's great, but my younger cousin is kind of a lot, so I was craving…"

You. Oh my God, I was craving you.

Daisy could feel his eyes on her, and she felt like her skin was alive. She wanted to grab him and kiss him. She wanted to strip his shirt off and run her hands over every inch of his skin.

The corner of Spider's mouth turned up. "You don't smoke."

"I've smoked." She tried to seem casual and tough.

"Maybe once or twice." Spider pushed away from the fence and approached her. He held his cigarette away from her as he leaned closer. He smelled faintly of sweat, cigarette smoke, and fresh laundry.

Daisy blinked. It was an unexpected smell for a man, one that reminded her of home and sunny afternoons with Tia Imelda.

"But you don't smoke." He said it like a statement.

"How can you tell?"

He glanced down, and Daisy wished she were wearing a different shirt, something cooler, not a ruffle-trimmed blouse she'd thought would look nice with her jeans.

"Fucking cute," he muttered.

Daisy blinked. "What?"

"Nothing." He tugged at her arm until she pulled her hand from her pocket. Then Spider lifted it and slid his thumb lazily from her palm up the inside of her fingers, parting the index and middle fingers with his own.

Oh. Daisy felt something inside her start to burn. *This is why people talk about sex so much.*

"Here." He teased the edge of her middle finger. "If you smoked, you'd have a tobacco stain here."

She didn't want to move, and she definitely didn't want to move her hand. She stared at his full lower lip and the defined line of his mouth. "I tried it once, but honestly, it tasted pretty gross."

"It's a disgusting habit."

She couldn't stop staring at his mouth. "So why do it?"

"I used to have other ones that were a lot worse." He released her hand. "So why'd you really come out here? 'Cause it wasn't to smoke."

"I'm supposed to get your phone number." She blurted the words in a Spider-induced haze, then realized what she'd said and looked up in panic. "I mean…"

He didn't look amused. "What was it? You win a bet? Or did you lose one?"

CHAPTER 4

SPIDER FELT the humiliation burning in his chest, but he didn't look away. She and her pretty little cousins had been giggling at the table, glancing at him and the guys from the tattoo shop. Then she'd followed him out here and he'd entertained the ridiculous thought that she'd come to talk to him.

It must have been some kind of challenge, some pretty-girl bet that she'd lost to get a number from the cholo at the bar.

Spider couldn't even be angry; she was clearly embarrassed to be there.

"They were teasing me." Daisy looked at the ground. "I don't date much, and they said something about you getting coffee at the café every day and I told them…" She stepped back. "I'm stupid. I'm sorry I—"

"You're not stupid."

She looked up. "What?"

"Everyone in town talks about how smart you are, how you're going off to a big college next year, so I know you're not stupid."

She stepped closer to him, and he was hit by the combination of vanilla and something spicy like cinnamon or cloves. She smelled like the café, and the café smelled like pie, and Spider couldn't decide if he wanted to run away or take a bite out of her.

You taste as good as you smell, princesa?

"Thanks." She smiled, and then she looked away. "Yeah, everyone is planning my great exit, including my two idiot cousins."

Something about the way she said it bothered him. "You don't want to go to college or something? I was just saying you're not stupid; I need to change my opinion on that?"

She lifted her chin, and a hint of fire came into her eyes. "You know, *you're* not stupid; I could tell by the way you talked to Emmie about doing her history home-work. So why do you have to go to college to be smart?"

"I'm not smart; I'm ignorant as fuck." Shit. He prob-ably shouldn't curse around her. "Listen, princesa, I don't know about Rome and that shit because I'm educated. I know about it because I'm fucking poor and I don't have a TV, so books are my only entertainment." He tossed the cigarette, which had burned out, and stepped back to light another one. "But you not going to college when you got the brains and the family to support you? That's fucking dumb."

Her mouth dropped open, and her eyes narrowed. Damn, it should not have been hot, but Spider had always had a weakness for women with a temper.

"Screw you," she said. "My dad didn't go to college, and he's smart. My tia Imelda didn't, and she's one of the most brilliant people I know. And I'm not a princess, okay?"

"I'm gonna guess they didn't exactly have the choices you have. You may say you're not a princess, but you got a chance to leave this little-ass town and go do something huge in the world, and you're acting like it's some kind of hardship?" Spider took a slow drag on his cigarette and blew out the smoke. "I mean, that's dumb as fuck."

She opened her mouth, then closed it. "I... I don't even know you."

Spider held out his hand. "Spider Villalobos. And you are?"

He knew who she was. Everyone knew who she was, but he enjoyed the look of confusion on her face.

"I'm Daisy."

He raised one eyebrow. "Daisy...?"

"Daisy Rivera. My family has Café Maya on Main— You know all this. You come in there every day!" She looked around, realizing she was practically yelling. "Listen, can I just get your phone number so my cousins will leave me alone? I promise I won't call you or anything, but it'll get them off my back."

"Oh right. The bet."

"It's not a bet! They know I think you're cute, and they're being obnoxious about it, and you know what?" She reached for a napkin on the nearby table. "Never mind, I'll make something up. Just forget we ever talked. Please—*please* forget this conversation ever happened."

Spider frowned.

They know I think you're cute.

Cute?

Spider didn't think anyone had ever called him cute.

Bad. Dangerous. Even hot or sexy sometimes. He'd heard those, and whatever, sexual attraction didn't follow any rules.

Cute?

He watched as she dug through her purse, clearly looking for a pen that she didn't have and slowly coming to the realization that she'd have to speak to him again.

Daisy sighed and closed her eyes. "Do you have a pen I can borrow?"

"You want to borrow a pen from me to write down a fake phone number to fool your cousins?"

It was as if she was shrinking in front of him, and the feeling filled him with a sudden punch of emotions. Shame and anger. Deep-seated, gut-curling anger.

She shouldn't shrink. Ever. Of all the things this woman shouldn't do, it was make herself small. For anyone, and especially not him.

Spider stubbed out his cigarette, reached for the pen he always kept in his back pocket, and then reached for Daisy's hand. "You like ink?"

She was staring again. "I don't have any tattoos."

"This'll wash off." He clicked his pen and tucked her warm little hand against his side and braced her forearm with his hand. "Little rubbing alcohol, little baby oil, and it'll be gone."

The pen was one of his good ones, and the ink flowed over her skin like oil on glass.

"I don't have my own phone," he said. "And I hate cell phones." He drew the first number with a flourish, then added curls and shading to the number, turning it from a cold digit into a small work of art. "And you really shouldn't be spending time with me because I'm not for you, princesa. It wouldn't be a good idea."

He kept his voice soft as he moved on to the second number, then the third. "But if you ever need help—if some asshole is ever bothering you—even if your car runs out of gas or some shit. Whatever, you know?" He finished the numbers and added a few extra details in the corner along with a small flower as sweet as she smelled. "Call this number and I'll be there, okay? Leave a message…" He blew on her skin to set the ink, then stepped back, holding her hand out for a long moment before he released her. "Get a message to me, and I'll find you."

Daisy's cheeks were pink, her mouth gaped a little, and it took every ounce of self-control to not grab her, sink his hand into her curls, and seduce the hell out of her. He could tell she was inexperienced with guys, and the temptation to open her eyes was gnawing at him.

39

Princesa, you have no idea.

"Thanks." She looked at her arm, then backed away, turned, and went inside.

Spider took his position on the back fence, lit another cigarette, and stared at the door where Daisy had disappeared.

Self-control.

He fucking had it.

————

SPIDER SKIPPED THE CAFÉ FOR A SOLID WEEK after talking with Daisy at the Ice House. He knew that seeing his ink on her skin would be a little too tempting, and he was hoping it would be gone or at least pretty faded by the time he walked into the place on Wednesday.

He wasn't going to completely deprive himself of her presence, but he knew he could only take small doses of Daisy Rivera. It was the same way he'd taken drugs when he was running with Chino. Spider knew he had to do some shit because otherwise he'd have stood out, but since he'd seen what that kind of garbage did to other people, he was careful.

He'd manage to avoid most of it by making his hands tremble violently the one time he took meth. Since no one wanted a tattoo artist with the shakes, he was allowed to skip most of the harder stuff that Chino pushed on the boys as long as he kept busy.

The morning was fresh and the sky a clear blue when he walked downtown. He wasn't working until two that afternoon, but he'd promised Betsy to help her pack some boxes at the bookstore. He could justify the coffee if he was helping with the books. Maybe Daisy was wearing that shirt with the ruffles again. He'd decided it was his new favorite.

Spider had carefully washed out the travel coffee mug that Betsy gave him the previous Christmas. It made the old lady smile every time she saw him use it, and hell, that thing kept coffee warm for fucking hours. It was amazing.

The bell rang as he pushed open the door, but there was no Daisy in sight. Instead, her aunt was at the register, sitting on a tall stool with a padded back and chatting with Ruby, his boss's wife.

"Spider!" Ruby grinned at him. She was in her midforties and a solid artist. "You switch shifts with someone?"

"Nah." He nodded toward the street. "I told Betsy I'd help her out with some heavy stuff."

"You're a sweetheart to help her." Ruby winked at him. "Don't worry; I won't tell the guys."

Spider liked working with Ruby because not only did she do good work, she didn't have an ego like most tattoo artists. Including him.

Yeah, he could admit it. His ego was fucking huge when it came to his ink. He was the best artist in Metlin, not that he could say that yet, but he knew he was. Hell, he'd been the best artist in LA when he was fifteen. Guys came from all over the city to have Spider tattoo them, and he wasn't just talking about the assholes in Chino's crew.

He stepped up to the counter and handed the old woman his travel mug. "Can I get a refill? Just black coffee please."

"I know what you drink, young man." She patted Spider's hand and glanced at Ruby. "I better get back to work, Miss Ruby. You be good."

"You too." Ruby headed toward the door. "See you later, Leg Man."

The older woman turned to frown at Ruby, but she was already gone. She turned her eyes to Spider. "Leg man?"

"Spider," he muttered. "'Cause they have lots of legs. I don't know, she thinks it's funny."

Daisy's aunt laughed a little. "That one has a strange sense of humor." She waved a hand. "A good person though."

"Yeah, she and Bill are great."

"You're living in that apartment over their garage, right? Their son's old room?"

"I think so; some of his stuff is still there."

"He's a nice boy, but now that he has a fancy job in Seattle, he's embarrassed by his parents." She shook her head. "What kind of child is embarrassed by their parents? They run an honest business."

Spider knew better than to talk shit about Ruby and

Bill's son. "I don't know anything about him, so I can't say."

The old woman set his coffee on the counter, and Spider noticed that there weren't many people in the café, which was probably why the lady seemed ready to strike up a conversation.

No sign of Daisy at all.

"Thanks, Mrs. Rivera. How much—?"

"Oh, I'm not a Rivera." She smiled. "That's Daisy's father's family. I'm her grandmother's sister. Just call me Tia Imelda."

"Tia..." Spider had never called anyone tia. Not even in his own family. He didn't know any of his aunts. "Okay, thanks. How much for the coffee?"

Imelda ignored him and asked, "What do your parents do?"

The wound was well and truly scarred over, so Spider didn't flinch. "Both my parents are dead." He opened his coffee and grabbed three sugar packets from the counter. "But my dad was a car upholsterer, and my mom was a housewife. Until my dad died; then she cleaned houses."

There had been a flash of pity, but that was why Spider kept talking. If you stopped talking at the dead-parents part, no one listened to anything else you said.

"See? Working people. And I don't see you being embarrassed by either of them."

"No, ma'am." Of course, he was a tattoo artist, not a financial analyst or whatever Ruby's kid was now.

But Spider could never be embarrassed by his

parents. He only wished his mother hadn't been embarrassed by *him* when she died. On good days, he thought maybe they could see him from heaven and be happy that he'd turned shit around. Now the challenge was keeping it that way.

Imelda was shaking a finger at him. "I think you have a beautiful old car, don't you? I've seen you drive it around town."

"The El Camino?"

"Yes! Was it your father's?"

Spider couldn't stop the smile. "Yeah. You like old cars?"

"Are you joking?" She pointed to a black-and-white photo behind the counter. "You know who that is?"

Spider leaned forward and examined the picture. There was a slick-looking pachuco in a black suit and a shiny black pompadour haircut with a low fade. On either side of him were two beautiful women: A curvaceous woman who looked more than a little like Daisy was standing with her hand at her waist, a scarf tied around her neck, wearing a halter-top dress and dark lipstick. The other woman was taller, with attitude to spare. She was leaning on the car and kicking up a pointed heel.

The group was standing in front of a very sweet car that was vintage 1940s American-manufacturing gold. The chrome made Spider want to drool.

"You were rocking those shades." He had a feeling he

was seeing Imelda in her prime. "And that car is insane. Is that a Buick?"

"You *do* know cars." She smiled. "That's a 1948 Buick Roadmaster Riviera. Maya and Enrique had only been married a few years, and I had come north for a visit. I thought it was so glamorous! Enrique said he had to get it because of the name. Rivera. Riviera. Maya called it his Roadmaster Rivera." The old woman laughed. "We took that picture in the fifties. My sister loved that car, and Enrique loved driving her in it. He kept it perfect."

"Enrique was Daisy's grandfather?"

"Órale, look at them, right? The most handsome couple you've ever seen in your life." She touched the simple frame. "Enrique and Maya knew how to dress, I can tell you that. And he was a genius with cars. He could fix anything. And Maya?" Imelda spread her hand toward the counter. "She could cook anything."

"Yeah, my mom and dad were the same way. He loved doing upholstery though. I guess his dad was like a… a camisero, you know? What's the word for guys who make suits?"

"A tailor," Imelda said. "He would have been a tailor."

"Yeah, a tailor." Spider nodded at the picture and looked at another formal portrait of Mr. and Mrs. Rivera that was framed on the wall. "Damn, everything was cool then, you know? The cars. The clothes." He heard the oldies station playing in the background. "The music."

"It was cool," Imelda said. "But harder. In a lot of ways, much harder. And not as many opportunities for us as you kids have now."

"What about you?" He picked up his coffee. "Did you ever get married or anything?"

"I never wanted to," Imelda said. "My sister and I came from a big family, and I liked my freedom, you know?"

Spider nodded. "I get that."

"But after my sister passed?" Imelda looked over her shoulder at the old photograph. "I realized that freedom doesn't mean much if you don't have people who love you."

Spider kept his eyes on the photo, imagining the life that the Riveras had and how quickly it had changed on them.

As fast as a bullet from a gun.

Spider took a sip of his coffee. "They'd be proud of Daisy, I bet. Getting such good grades, going to a big college."

"Enrique and Maya were proud of both their kids, but mostly that they knew how to work and how to take care of their family, you understand?" She glanced at Spider from the corner of her eye. "That's what we were taught. Education is important, but getting a diploma in school doesn't teach you how to take care of people. And that's one of the most important skills to learn for anyone, don't you think?"

He turned to her and nodded. "Yes, ma'am."

She reached up and patted his cheek. "I'm sure your parents are very proud of you too. I can see how hard you work. Even when you come in to stare at my niece."

Oh shit. "Tia Imelda—"

"Did I say I minded?" She smiled and wrote a note in a pad by the counter. "She's not working today. Meeting with her school counselor, I think. They want her to fill out the applications to go away next year." Imelda blinked. "I don't know what I'll do without her. Her mother runs the business so well, but Daisy is the only one who wanted to learn all the old recipes."

"She won't forget them; she's too smart for that." He had months at most. Months that he could enjoy her smile and see her face. He was going to start drinking way more coffee.

He might have to switch to decaf.

"I guess you're right." Imelda walked over and opened the pastry case before she folded a bright pink box and bent over. "You know, a lot of people see Daisy's *accomplishments*." She added two twisted cinnamon breads to the box. "But a person's accomplishments aren't who they are. They're just the things they've done." She added two more flaky turnovers, then straightened and closed the box. "I think you see though."

"See what?"

She slid the box across the top of the glass case. "You're not a superficial person, Spider. She needs someone who sees who she is, not just what she's done."

Spider opened his mouth, but nothing came out for a long minute. "I don't think I'm the right—"

"You can take these pastries to Betsy, can't you? I'd really appreciate it." The old woman climbed back up on her stool. "With Daisy gone, I have to stay at the register. I'll throw in your coffee as a delivery fee, yeah?"

Spider gave up. "Sure. And thanks." He grabbed the box and headed toward the door.

"And Spider?"

"Yeah?"

"Maya's husband, Enrique?" Her eyes twinkled. "He wasn't always an angel. How do you think they got the money to start the café?"

Spider's eyes went wide.

"It doesn't matter where you come from," the old woman said. "It matters where you're going and how you treat people along the way."

Arrieros somos y en el camino andamos.

It was one of his father's favorite sayings. He hadn't thought about that in years.

Spider raised the pastry box. "Thanks for this. I'll make sure Betsy gets it."

CHAPTER 5

DAISY NODDED as the guidance counselor droned on about course requirements, grade point averages, and financial aid packages. She idly traced the fading ink on her forearm, which was currently covered by a cardigan to combat the chill in the college's counseling office.

She wondered if a message to Spider was warranted for boredom.

"Please tell Spider I need him to rescue me from calculus requirements."

"I'm going to need an intervention to keep me from killing my advanced sociology professor."

"Let him know that my physics teacher is harassing me. And by harassing, I mean trying to teach me physics."

She blinked when she heard a hard clap. She blinked and looked up.

"Daisy?" Her counselor, Mr. Talbot, was looking at

her with concern. "Are you feeling all right? Should we reschedule?"

"No." Daisy shook her head. "No, I'm sorry I'm distracted. I had kind of a weird weekend."

"Well, you should have been having a great one considering your schedule. You're sailing through your general education. Have you thought any more about where you want to submit your transfer applications?"

Does it matter? All the colleges her parents wanted for her were hundreds of miles from Metlin. "What about Fresno?"

Mr. Talbot looked disappointed. "Daisy, you'll have your pick of schools. Don't limit yourself because of geography. You're going to be eligible for a number of financial aid packages because... Well, you qualify for a lot."

Because she was the first in her family to attend a university, there were all sorts of financial aid packages available to her. Even though both her parents had very successful businesses. Something about it rubbed Daisy the wrong way.

"Mr. T, what about a gap year?" Maybe she could convince her parents to just let her work for a while. "I've been going to school for fifteen years straight. Plus summer programs. When you think about it—"

"I'd think you'd be eager to grab these opportunities." Mr. Talbot interrupted her. "You've grown up here and haven't traveled much. There are many avenues that are going to open up to you when you're in the state university system. Travel opportunities, international scholarships, internships once you decide where you want to major."

"I'm still thinking business. Or marketing." At least those were classes she could use at the café. "Mr. T, did you go to school?"

"I did!" The man smiled broadly. "I graduated twenty years ago next spring."

"And what did you study?"

His smile faltered. "Um… art history. You see, at the time—"

"But you like what you do, right?" Daisy was trying to prove a point, one she thought might work on her parents. "I mean, it's obvious you really love what you do." It was true, Mr. Talbot was one of her biggest supporters and encouragers, and she knew he was like that with all the students he saw. Despite her mood that day, she knew he was a great guidance counselor.

"I do love what I do." Mr. Talbot beamed. "I love working with students, and I'm very glad you can see that."

"I definitely can. Plus you're really good at it. You've helped me plan my schedule so well that I'm nearly all done with my general education, and I've been in school less than two years."

"It helped that you started taking college courses in high school."

"Still, you love what you do, but it's not what you studied in college. Maybe…" She shrugged. "I mean, if you already know what you want to do in life, should you really go to college? If doing that thing you love doesn't *require* a college degree?"

Mr. Talbot's smile fell. "Daisy, are you thinking about *not* transferring to a university?"

Yes! She couldn't say it. "I mean... it's more of a philosophical question, I guess. I'm just saying—"

"Are there..." Mr. Talbot's eyes drifted down to Daisy's stomach. "...*personal* reasons you might have to delay getting your education?" His voice was nearly a whisper.

"Oh my God, do you think I'm pregnant?" Daisy's eyes went wide. "Why would you say that?"

"I'm not... I don't..." Mr. Talbot sighed. "Daisy, I just don't understand why you would want to put off your education. You're bright and so talented. You could study anything. Psychology, business, premed. Literally, your grades are good in *everything*."

She could study anything, except... the thing she really wanted to do. Stay in Metlin and run the family café.

Daisy grabbed the stack of papers off Mr. Talbot's desk and stood. "I'm going to take all this home and look over everything. I'll call you in a couple of weeks to talk about where to send my applications. I have time, right?"

"Most deadlines are the end of November." Mr. Talbot looked relieved that Daisy had picked up the paperwork. "You've got plenty of time."

She was nearly crying by the time she reached her car. She stuffed her books and backpack in the trunk and slammed it shut. Then she leaned on her trunk, put her face in her hands, and drew in a ragged breath.

Yarn. She needed yarn.

———

DAISY STROLLED THROUGH THE AISLES OF THE big-box craft store and tried not to feel guilty. Tompkins Notions, the locally owned craft store downtown, didn't have a great selection of yarn since it focused more on sewing than fiber crafts. With the emotional storm she was fending off, Daisy just wanted to be surrounded by masses and masses of yarn.

She wandered up and down the aisle, looking at acrylic, cotton, and fancy wools. She briefly flirted with a cream-colored alpaca skein before she remembered she lived in Metlin, California, and it rarely dropped below freezing.

She fondled bouclés and chenilles. She stroked ribbon and poked at bright fringe.

A solid hour of yarn therapy netted her three skeins for Christmas knitting and a fancy bouclé to make Imelda a scarf. She was juggling the yarn and trying to read a pattern hung on an end cap when she bumped into someone.

"Oh, I am so sorr—" She gasped when she saw who it was. "Spider?"

"Daisy."

He was standing stock-still, a red basket clutched in one hand. His eyes raked over her, from her very unsexy sneakers to her faded jeans to the messy bun that probably still had a pencil or two sticking out of it.

He was frowning. "What are you doing here? Your aunt said you had a meeting at your school."

"You asked my aunt where I was?"

"You weren't at the café."

"Neither were you." She'd noticed. "Not for, like, a week."

He glanced away. "I was kind of... busy."

"Right."

He looked at the bundle in her arms. "Yarn?"

"Yeah, well, it wasn't such a great day so... yarn."

He frowned. "Why?"

"I like yarn. What are you doing here?" She glanced at his basket. "Oh, art supplies. That makes sense."

"Bill asked me to put some flash on the walls by my station," he muttered. "Just some stuff I'd be willing to do for the college-girl crowd, you know? I mostly do custom stuff, but I'm working more hours now."

"College-girl crowd?" Daisy felt her temper prick. "Like me?"

He smiled a little. "Not like you. I mean... yeah, you're in college, but I'm talking about—"

"You're talking about silly girls who wander into the shop when they're drunk or partying with their friends or having a birthday, right?"

He narrowed his eyes. "I guess so. Though, to be clear, I do not tattoo drunk people. I have ethics and shit."

She ignored him. She could feel her face heating up with the indignities of the day. "So these college girls will come in, and you'll tell them to pick out the prettiest butterfly or bird and you'll put it on their wrist or their back or their shoulder." Her fingers gripped the yarn. "And you'll do a good job, but then as soon as they leave with their friends, you'll make fun of those silly girls, right?"

Spider carefully set his basket of pencils and paper down before he crossed his arms. "You're making a lot of assumptions, princesa."

"But am I wrong? You and the entire shop—the entire rest of the world—will make fun of their pretty butterflies or birds or that special quote from their favorite poet. Because it's not big and tough and cool like..." She roughly gestured to his arms. "*That*. It's not edgy like skulls or bloody crosses. Because butterflies and birds are just *girl* things, and we don't take girl things seriously, do we?"

Spider kept his gaze level. "Who made fun of you, Daisy?"

"Everyone, okay?" She threw her arms out and tossed her yarn in a nearby basket. "Everyone makes fun of the things I like. Whether it's knitting or gardening or... or baking. Who cares about that stuff, right? That's like... housewife stuff. It's not *important* like psychology or finance or medicine. I mean, why would I want to run a bakery when I could go be a psychologist? Didn't you say it? That would be *dumb*."

He furrowed his eyebrows together. "I didn't—"

"That's what you said. That's what you think. I get it." She put her fist on her hips. "I get that it's not what everyone thinks I should be doing, but you know what? I've been telling people for years what I actually want and they all treat me just like you treat those silly college girls who come into the tattoo shop. Like they're immature children who don't really know what they want and aren't ready for real life."

She stepped closer to Spider and looked up. "I do know what I want. And I don't think it's silly or dumb to like beautiful things. I *like* butterflies and birds and rainbows. I *like* poetry and soft things and—"

Daisy was cut off by a flash of heat, hands, and motion as Spider put one hand on her cheek as his other arm slipped around her waist, pulling her up and into his chest. His mouth landed on hers, and his fingers slid back into her hair, tilting her lips until they aligned with his.

He didn't kiss her; he *took* her.

Spider took her breath, her anger, and every thought from her head. She reached her arms up and gripped his neck, drawing him closer as his hand fell from her cheek and slid around her waist, his fingers spreading wide at the small of her back to press her belly into his.

She could feel the rock-hard muscle he hid under his

shirt, the solid plane of his abdomen, his chest pressing against her breasts.

Daisy felt her entire body soften as Spider backed her into one of the yarn displays. She barely registered the pinch of metal against her back as he continued to ravish her mouth.

She could feel the ache between her thighs, the solid erection hidden behind his jeans. His hand slipped down and cupped the curve of her ass, and she let out an incoherent sound that was somewhere in the neighborhood of a cat.

Spider lifted his head and his hand froze. "I'm sorry, I should have asked—"

"Yes." She pulled his mouth back to hers. *Yes yes yes yes—*

"EXCUSE ME!"

Daisy's eyes went wide. Spider froze with Daisy halfway sitting in a basket of chenille, one hand on her butt and the other hooked under her thigh.

"This. Is not. The place. For *that*." A beige-colored woman with lifeless grey hair and a blue apron glared at them. "Please leave."

Daisy's face burned. It could have been funny. If this had happened at Tompkins, Trudi would have teased Daisy and threatened to tell her cousins about Spider kissing her in the middle of the store after she'd been ranting about yarn and butterfly tattoos.

But they weren't downtown.

Everything about the beige woman, from her derisive

glare to her curled lip to the way she looked down her nose, told Daisy what she thought of them.

Cool as could be, Spider lowered Daisy to her feet, reached down for his basket, and casually tossed her four skeins of yarn in it along with another of the black chenille that she'd been sitting in.

Daisy decided not to mention it.

Then Spider reached out, took her hand, and walked toward the woman, who opened her mouth to protest until he stopped less than a foot from her, staring down into her face.

The woman shut her mouth.

"My girl and I were just checking out." Spider didn't move, daring the woman to say something.

She got her courage back, just a little. "Well, I'm telling you to—"

"Check out?" He cocked his head and stared at her, his dark eyes drilling into her glare.

It was the first time Daisy had seen Spider the way she knew others must see him all the time. Inked to the neck, baggy jeans, and black boots, his hair a close-cropped black velvet with terrifying legs threatening to emerge from the darkness.

He was... scary.

"Let's go." She squeezed his hand. "Let's get our stuff and go."

"Thank you for doing business at Hobby Hut," Spider said softly. "Isn't that what you're supposed to say?"

Daisy tugged his hand. "Please, let's go."

Spider didn't take his eyes off the woman until Daisy tugged him away. He stepped past her and walked to the front of the store, where he checked out with a white-haired lady who looked amused by the whole thing and called Spider "sugar."

Spider put his art supplies in one bag and her yarn in a separate one, then carried both of them and took Daisy's hand, staring down the beige woman who lingered near the front of the store, waiting for them to leave.

As they passed her, Daisy paused. "Women like you give home arts a bad name." She lifted her chin. "Shame on you."

There was a hoot in the background along with the sound of laughter. Then Daisy and Spider walked to the parking lot and didn't look back.

"I think I better stick to buying yarn at Tompkins from now on."

"Yarn." Spider shook his head. "Princesa, you're gonna have to explain that one to me."

CHAPTER 6

SPIDER DROVE BACK to his apartment, glancing every five seconds at the blue Honda Civic in his rearview mirror.

What the fuck are you doing, asshole?

He was an idiot. She'd been lonely and sad and indignant all at the same time, pushing every one of his buttons. He wanted to protect her, beat up any bastard who dared disrespect her, and then work the mad out of her in every hot and sweaty way he could imagine.

You're an idiot.

Now Daisy was probably banned from buying yarn at her favorite store and he'd probably get the cops called on him for threatening Our Constipated Lady of the Cockblock. He glanced at the bag of art supplies and mentally cursed out Bill for telling him they were cheaper at Hobby Hut instead of going to Mancini Art Supply downtown.

Sure, he'd saved a little money, but no one at Mancini's looked at him like he was a cockroach.

He stopped in front of the alley gate and dragged open the door before he pulled the El Camino into the asphalt driveway at the back of Bill and Ruby's place. Then he waved Daisy in, and she managed to wedge her little compact car behind his with just enough room to close the gate.

She got out as he was securing the latch. "This is where you live?"

He pointed to the apartment over the garage. "I have my own entrance, so it's cool. And if Bill and Ruby go anywhere, I feed their dogs for them."

"What about if you go somewhere?" She was looking around. "Do you have any pets?"

Spider wanted to get a cat, but he'd decided it was a bad idea. "Where the hell am I going to go?" He put his hand on the small of her back and ushered her toward the stairs before anyone saw her. "Come on. You thirsty?"

What the fuck are you going to offer her, asshole?

Too late, he realized that his choices to get Daisy a drink were water or milk. She was already walking through his door, a silly little smile on her face that made him want to kiss her again.

Fuck, she tasted so good. Her mouth had tasted like mint and her lip gloss had been vanilla or some shit like that because when he licked his lips after he kissed her, it tasted like a muffin. Where the hell did girls even find stuff like that?

"I like your place." She was looking around at his bedroom. "It's really… clean."

He nodded. "Yeah. I like to keep things organized."

She bit the corner of her lip. "I can tell."

Spider didn't own a chair. The sole surface for sitting was his full-size bed, but that didn't seem like a very good option if he was trying to get control of his dick.

Of course, the only other option was the floor.

"Um…" He gestured to the corner of the bed. "Sit. I'll get you some water. Or milk. Sorry, I don't have anything else. I'm not used to—"

"Spider." Daisy was looking around, and her expression was amused. Not like mocking amused, just sweet. 'Cause she was a fucking sweetheart. "It's pretty obvious you weren't expecting company. It's okay. Why don't we go get a coffee or something? We don't have to hide here."

She thought they should be seen together? In public? "I don't think that's a good idea."

"Why?"

'Cause I'm a fucking homeboy and you're a decent girl. He shook his head. "Daisy, I like you—"

"I like you too." Her cheeks were a little pink. "And I'm not embarrassed to be seen with you. Are you embarrassed by me?"

"Embarrassed by *you*?" He snorted. "That's not the way this works, princesa. I'm the embarrassing one, remember? You're Metlin's golden girl. The last thing your reputation needs is someone like me—"

"My reputation?" She stood and laughed a little. "Spider, it's not 1965. I don't have to worry about my *reputation*." She looked out a window. "I think you're embarrassed. Dating one of those silly college girls you and the guys—"

"If you fucking insult yourself, you're gonna make me crazy." His voice was low. "Do you really want to get grief from your family about me when you're already kind of fighting with them about the school thing?"

That shut her up. She sat on the edge of the bed, still staring out the window.

"Daisy, I think you're smart and funny and sexy as hell. Obviously, since I'm willing to get kicked out of public places for making out with you, that should not be a question." He knelt in front of her. "But think about this, okay?"

She locked eyes with him, and the sight of her— wide-eyed and sitting on the edge of his bed like a sexy librarian or some shit with a pencil stuck in her hair— would have driven him to his knees if he hadn't been there already.

"You are gorgeous, princesa. And I'm not just talking about your looks. You're smart and bright and you make everybody around you feel good. Half the people who walk into your café go there just so they can get one of your smiles. You care about people, Daisy. You're a good person, and I know whatever you do in life is gonna be a success. If you become a doctor or a psychologist or—"

"I don't want any of those things. I want to stay in Metlin and run the café. I told you that."

"You can always do that if you want, you know? But just... get the degree first. Life is..." He thought about his mom, so happy to be a wife and mom, making their home a sanctuary before his father died. "Life can get fucked up. If you have a college degree, that's a pretty big advantage, you know? You'll always have that even if shit goes down."

She squeezed his hands. "I promise I will think about what you said. But none of this has anything to do with us dating. I like you. You like me. What's the problem?"

"Daisy, I have never really wondered about your eyesight before this, but have you seen my fucking neck?"

"I like your neck." She ran his fingers along his collarbone, and it took everything in Spider not to lay his head in her lap like a starving dog.

"You shouldn't like my neck. I was in a fucking gang. It's not a good thing. It's not a romantic thing. It's ugly and violent and kills everything good. Please don't think this is cool."

"I don't think it's cool." She kept her hand on his neck, the tips of her fingers hovering right over his pulse. "I also don't think it's the end of the world. You were in a gang."

"Yes."

"I'm guessing you joined pretty young."

"You could say that." Chino's boys had jumped him in weeks after his father's death. In retrospect, it was really fucked up.

"And are you still in a gang?"

"Fuck no. Not since I was seventeen."

"Okay." She shrugged. "So we can date."

He stood and knit his hands together behind his neck, trying not to growl. "That's not the way this works. It's not that easy."

"It's not that easy because you're making it difficult." She stood and put her hand on his shoulder.

Spider stilled. His arms fell to his sides, and his palms came to rest on Daisy's soft hips. He didn't even feel like he was controlling his own body. She came to him, and he responded. Done and done.

Daisy slid a single finger along his jaw. "I think we should try dating. If you just want to meet here, that's cool for now. I don't want anyone to freak out, especially you."

"Okay."

What the fuck? No, not okay! What the hell was he saying?

"When you're ready to hang out with me at the Ice House or something, we can do that. There's no rush."

No rush? Spider was going to take this so fucking slow a glacier was going to look speedy. There was no way he was moving fast with Daisy Rivera. He'd be giving her plenty of time to come to her senses.

"Okay." He nodded. "No rush."

Her smile was brilliant. "Good."

She lifted onto her toes and met his hungry mouth with a sweet kiss. This time he kept a short leash on his reaction. He slowly explored her lips and kept his hands planted on her hips. No roaming. No copping a feel.

After all, in less than a year she'd be going away for college anyway. Until then, he could make her feel good. Be sweet to her. Show her how she should be treated when she met a decent guy later.

He could do that. It would be... educational.

———

Hours after Daisy had left for a shift at the café, Spider was working on his flash at Bill and Ruby's place, sketching out some fucking awesome butterflies.

"...butterflies and birds are just girl things, and we don't take girl things seriously, do we?"

She was right, and it made him feel like shit. He did think less of the young women who came into the shop and picked out a pretty picture to go on their shoulder or their ankle. He did fall into the "good-natured" jokes about birds and rainbows.

But seriously, what the fuck was wrong with birds and rainbows?

Was that any less original than the eight hundred tattoos of the Sacred Heart or bloody daggers or gap-toothed skulls he'd tattooed on dudes over the years? What was wrong with some fucking positivity?

Fuck the haters, Spider had decided. Butterflies and birds were fucking awesome, and he was going to make the best goddamn flash those college girls had ever seen. He wasn't going to just ink butterflies, he was gonna ink fucking awesome butterflies.

'Cause his girl liked butterflies, and she had a damn good point.

"Hey, Spider?" Bill called from across the shop. "Can I talk to you for a minute?"

Spider looked up and froze. Oh shit. Had Bill seen Daisy's car at his place? Had Ruby seen it and told Imelda? "Yeah, boss. Let me just clean this up."

He meticulously organized the finished drawings into one pile, the sketches into another, and his blank pages into another. Then he quickly put his pencils in the case, making sure to organize them by weight before he snapped the lid closed and slid them next to his acrylics.

Spider was renting from Bill, but it wasn't like they had a contract or anything. He paid cash and he didn't have a lease. Bill could kick Spider out at any time. Was he going to fire him? He didn't think Bill would fire him for dating the Rivera's daughter, but there was no telling. Ruby and Imelda were tight.

Tia Imelda didn't mind that you like Daisy.

Yeah, there was looking and then there was reality. Tias could be romantics; parents, not so much.

He followed Bill back into the bookkeeping office

where Ruby was usually tapping away on the computer. Today Ruby wasn't there, and Bill shut the door behind them.

His boss was a barrel-chested man with bright white hair that was slicked back and a full beard that fell to his chest. He looked like an old biker because he was one. Spider didn't think Bill was in an MC, but he probably knew guys who were, which was always why Spider had assumed Bill was cool about not asking too many questions about his past.

"Everything okay?" Spider tried not to panic.

Bill motioned him toward a chair. "Sit down, son. I wanted to ask the same thing about you."

"Why?" Spider gripped the arms of his chair. "Did you hear something?"

"You know Manuel Jimenez out in Oakville?"

"I heard of him." Oakville was a small community in the foothills east of Metlin. "He's a pretty good artist, I hear."

"Good guy too." Bill stroked his beard. "Couple of guys came out to Manuel's place asking about you."

"About me?"

Bill nodded. "Manuel's your given name, right? The one on your state license?"

Spider felt his heart start to pound. "Yeah, it is." And now a couple of guys were coming around another Manuel's place, looking for a tattoo artist named Spider. "They cause any problems for Manuel?"

Bill frowned and shook his head. "Nah, he's fine. Didn't even faze him; he's cool."

Spider shifted in his seat. "Did he—?"

"Didn't say anything to them about you. He knows you're one of my guys."

The ball of tension in his chest loosened a little, but it didn't unknot. "Do I need to take off?" There was a drumbeat in his head. He could be gone in fifteen minutes. Five minutes to run to the apartment, ten minutes to pack and be gone.

"Do you *want* to take off?" Bill leaned forward. "I know you don't have a record because I checked. Is there anything outstanding—?"

"I haven't done anything other than working off the books since I was seventeen." Spider looked him in the eye. "Nothing, I promise."

"Anyone out there looking for revenge or some shit like that?"

"No." He folded his hands. "It wouldn't be for revenge. I didn't steal anything. I don't owe anyone nothing. It's just… I didn't ask permission, you know? To leave."

Because no one was ever going to give Spider permission to exit gang life. It didn't work that way.

"I see." Bill sat back. "Do you want to leave town? If you need cash, I can pay you in advance."

Spider looked at Bill's kind expression and suddenly realized the man looked like Santa Claus. No wonder his grandkids were nuts about him.

Spider looked at his hands; he'd covered the worst of the scars with ink, but they were still there underneath. "I don't *want* to leave, but I don't want to make trouble for you or anyone else, you know?"

He thought about Betsy and Emmie first. Emmie wouldn't understand; Betsy would. Bill and Ruby. Frank Juarez, the rancher who'd hired him at Betsy's request, no questions asked. Mrs. Juarez still made tamales for Spider at Christmas.

Daisy. Fucking Daisy Rivera.

Princesa, I told you it wouldn't work.

"Hey, man." Bill leaned forward and drummed his fingers on the desk. "As far as I know, no one has come to Metlin looking around. I'd know if anyone was asking. Why don't you just wait and see, okay? Take it easy. Lie low—not like you don't do that already, but maybe don't hang at the Ice House with the guys for a while. Let me put out some feelers and see what comes back."

"Bill, I don't want anyone coming round here and—"

"Man." Bill grinned. "I'm not scared of these dudes. They don't want to mess with an old man who donates to the police retirement fund, you know what I mean?"

Bill donated to the police retirement fund? "Yeah." He was still feeling wary about sticking around, but Bill was right. If you were gonna get in a fight, it was always better to be in a neighborhood you knew.

And right now his neighborhood was Metlin.

CHAPTER 7

IT HAD BEEN a week since Daisy had visited Spider's apartment, and she was nearly jumping out of her skin. He'd called the café the day before and told her to come over that night around seven if she wanted a date.

What did he have planned? From the few minutes she'd spent in his place, it didn't even look like the man owned a chair. There had been a bed, a bookshelf, and various pieces of workout equipment carefully organized near what looked like a closet.

The studio had room for a small kitchen area and even a couch, but Spider had none of those things. He had a calendar on the wall from Metlin Auto Haus and a prayer card of Saint Luke from the local parish in the kitchen over the sink.

That was it.

She knew he had a personality, but it definitely wasn't reflected in his space. Daisy, who decorated the interior of her ten-year-old Honda Civic, was trying not to be horrified. The man desperately needed a picture frame or something.

She wondered if he'd object to her bringing him a plant.

Her little brother nudged her foot beneath the table. "Earth to Daisy."

"What?"

Kiko, her overgrown teenage brother, leaned over. "You're staring at the rice like it holds the secrets of the universe, Lazy Daze."

"Shut up." She shoved Kiko's elbow off the table. "Don't be rude."

He dropped his voice. "Are you thinking about your secret boyfriend?"

Daisy's eyes went wide and she stared at him. "What?"

"Oh shit!" He hooted, but he kept his voice to a whisper. "That means you have one. What the heck?"

"Be quiet." She stepped on his foot to shut him up.

They were sitting at Sunday dinner with the family, and their dad and Uncle Ray were currently discussing why two-by-four prices had gone up while their mom was debating with her oldest sister whether it would be better for Daisy to pick a school in the mountains or near the beach.

God help her.

Kiko kept his voice low. "You're twenty—why are you keeping your boyfriend a secret?"

"I don't have a secret boyfriend. Shut up." Daisy knew Kiko wouldn't just buy that. "It's, like, a new thing." She kept her voice low. "He's a *maybe* boyfriend and he's cool, but I don't want everyone giving me shit about it, you know? If it gets serious, I'll tell you." She squeezed his knee. "Tell anyone and I'll mess with your shampoo."

Kiko had gorgeous curly black hair like their father, and he was mildly obsessed with scalp health. "Damn, Daze. I'm not a punk. We're not little kids anymore, you know? I understand privacy."

She raised an eyebrow. "Oh yeah? What secrets are you hiding?"

His smile was more than a little smug. "If I told you, they wouldn't be secrets, would they?"

Daisy cocked her head and examined the little punk who was a foot taller than her now. "Okay, keep your secrets, but if it's anything important, you better tell me first."

"I promise." He leaned over and kissed the top of her head. "If I need any help, I will tell you, but it's cool. Promise."

She smiled. "Good. And if I need any help with the new guy, I'll tell you. But he's very nice to me."

"He better be," Kiko muttered, flexing his chest. "I've been lifting."

"Clearly." She poked his bicep and tried not to imagine her brother in a fight with Spider. The likely outcome would be laughably quick.

"Daisy!" her mom called. "We're completely leaving you out of this. Have you thought about whether you want to be near the beach, mija?" Her mom was glowing with the possibilities. "The weather is always so nice if you're by the coast, and I think it would be so fun, don't you think?"

Her Aunt Rosa countered. "But if she's spending all her time at the beach, is she going to be studying? I don't think it should factor in. Whichever school has the best program for what she wants to study—Daisy, what are you thinking about that?"

"Uh..." She hated this conversation. "I'm thinking more and more about business actually."

Her aunt and her mother clearly didn't love that idea.

"What about medicine?" Rosa asked. "You've always had such a calm presence and you do all those knitting things and the fancy pastries. You're good with your hands; I bet you'd make an excellent surgeon."

Her mother loved that. "Oh, I've never even thought about that, Rose, but you're right. She spends so much time making all those little cakes."

"They're called petits fours," Daisy tried to interject. "Or mignardises. They're a really advanced pastry. People in culinary school—"

"So if you can do those, then surgery— Oh!" Her mother turned to Rosa again. "And the sewing! Daisy makes all those beautiful clothes, and surgeons have to sew, right? Like, really fine stitching?"

"Plastic surgery." Rosa put a hand over her heart.

"She could work on one of those ships that does reconstructive surgery for children in poor countries." Rosa turned to her. "Daisy, you'd be so good at that."

Maybe she should just give up. They were right, she could probably make it through medical school, and helping kids was good, right? I mean, at the bakery she was just helping people get through the day with coffee and pie. Surgery for poor children was probably more important than coffee and pie.

So why did it make her feel so depressed?

She headed over to Spider's, feeling significantly deflated. She had one more week to finish her transfer applications for the following fall semester, and she was dragging her feet. She'd filled most of them out, but she hadn't submitted them, which was by far the easiest step.

He opened the door, smelling like clean linen and some kind of aftershave that made her think of fresh air and the mountains. She wanted to fall into his chest and sniff him like a puppy, but that would be weird.

"Hey!" He lifted her chin, and she had to look away from the spot on his chest where she wanted to bury her nose. "You all right?"

"Yeah." She took off her purse and jacket and handed them to him. "I just came from Sunday dinner with everyone, so—"

"Oh damn." He frowned. "You tired? We can hang out another time."

"No." She lifted her face, hoping he would kiss her. "I'm glad I'm here."

"Good." His smile was slow and sweet. "You smell like chile verde."

She let her head fall back. She'd changed her clothes, but there was no way to escape the smell of roasted chiles in her hair. "Oh my God. That's what I get for volunteering in the kitchen. The perfume of pork and green chiles."

Spider laughed and buried his face in her neck, kissing her just below her ear. "Smells good, princesa."

Daisy's heart skipped a beat. She braced her hand on his shoulder and her fingers dug in when his kisses slowly trailed up her neck, along the line of her chin, until he captured her mouth.

Damn, he was really good at this.

There was nothing awkward about kissing Spider. The boys she'd kissed before? Clearly rank amateurs compared to this man. He seemed to know exactly what angle to tilt her head and just how deep to make a kiss. It never felt gross or invasive. She just wanted more.

It was too soon when he pulled away and cleared his throat. "Okay, we better stop."

Or not. Daisy opened her eyes. They could *not* stop. That would be okay too.

"What do you think of my place?"

Daisy hadn't even noticed, but now she looked

around. "Spider! You got a chair." She grinned. "This looks great."

He must have been busy that week, because he'd not only gotten a chair, he'd actually put together a small dining set with a card table and two matching chairs. It was a little scuffed on the legs, but he'd also found a bright yellow cloth to cover it, and a clutch of white daisies sat in a clear glass.

"You got my flowers." Warmth filled her chest. "That's so..." Sweet? Adorable. He probably wouldn't appreciate those words. "...cool. So cool." She grabbed his hand.

"Yeah." He looked a little embarrassed. "I'm glad you like them." He turned. "I kind of changed the bed around."

"It looks great." She noticed another addition. "And you got a TV!"

"Bill had an extra one, so he let me have it. The DVD player works and everything."

"That's awesome." She took his hand and knit their fingers together.

On the top of the bookshelf, an old-fashioned square television sat. It had a built-in DVD player on the bottom of the unit and the screen was small, but it was in good condition.

"It's not hooked up to cable or anything," Spider said. "But Bill's son has a bunch of DVDs in the closet, so we can watch a movie if you want. I didn't get a couch cause I'm not sure how I'd get one up the stairs, but we can sit on the bed."

Spider had turned his bed to sit lengthwise against the wall and stacked pillows along the back, creating a kind of wide sofa perfect for lounging.

Daisy tried not to blush, thinking about lying in bed with Spider. "It looks perfect. Really comfortable."

"And I promise" —the corner of his mouth turned up — "I won't get... uh, carried away."

Daisy pursed her lips. "I mean, it's not a yarn store, so I think we'll be able to control ourselves."

Spider's half smile turned into a grin. "We can try."

Or not!

Daisy pursed her lips and looked around. "Did you do this for me?"

The apartment was still pretty spare, and there weren't any pictures on the walls, but it definitely looked more like an apartment and less like a cell.

"Yeah." He tried to play it off. "I mean, it was probably time for me to, like, fix up the place and everything."

Daisy couldn't ignore the spread of warmth in her chest. He'd made his apartment nice for her. She was definitely getting him a plant. Maybe a macramé wall hanging. Or a cross-stitch.

Spider walked to the small fridge and opened it. "I have orange and lime Jarritos in here. Then I got a Coke and a root beer too." He turned to her. "I saw you drinking the root beer at Ice House, so I figured that might be your favorite, but I didn't know."

"Root beer sounds perfect."

"Cool." He reached for the glasses over the sink. "Why don't you pick out a movie and we can watch it?"

They ended up settling on *The Godfather* since they had time before Daisy needed to get home, and most of the movies in the DVD case were either mafia movies, horror —which neither of them liked—or mindless action movies.

"You know, I've never actually seen this one," Spider said. "But it's, like, one of the greatest movies ever, right?"

"It's supposed to be really good." Daisy slipped off her shoes and settled into the stack of pillows along the wall. "I haven't seen it either. My mom never let us watch violent stuff."

"Sounds like my mom." As the movie started, Spider lifted the table and brought it to the side of the bed so they could set their drinks on it. "The music is boss."

He took off his shoes and sat next to her, bringing his arm around the back of her shoulders and pulling her toward him.

Heaven. She was in heaven.

The soaring music gave way to a quiet scene with a man who was more than a little hard to understand, but Daisy managed to make out most of the dialogue.

"Oh daaaaaamn." Spider set down his drink and pointed at the screen. "I have seen this. Or maybe just this scene." He was nodding along. "Make him an offer he can't refuse. Shit yeah, I seen this."

He sat back and drew Daisy under his arm again. "I don't usually watch mafia shit, princesa. But I know this is supposed to be good."

"I thought most guys loved all the mafia stuff. My brother is, like, obsessed with it."

Spider was quiet for a long time, but Daisy thought he was just focused on the movie.

"They put nice suits on and they drive kick-ass cars, but it's just a gang. In the end, the mafia is like any other gang." Spider pointed to the screen. "I promise you. All these people? They're all gonna die or they're gonna ruin their lives and lose everything good they ever had. Or the movie's bullshit."

Daisy looked at him, then leaned over and placed a soft kiss on his jaw. "Next time I'll bring some movies, okay? Something Bill's son didn't pick."

"I'm sure it's still a good movie, you know?" Spider hugged her closer. "Important art and all that."

"Know what else is important art? Romantic comedies."

"Fuck yeah, they are." He smiled. "You see *My Big Fat Greek Wedding*? Betsy had to make me watch it, but that shit's hilarious."

"*10 Things I Hate About You*," Daisy said. "A classic of American cinema."

"Fucking love that movie." He stared at the screen as ominous men in stylish hats offered dire warnings.

"Patrick Verona is the man. Next movie night is *10 Things I Hate About You*."

"Done." Daisy nuzzled under his jaw and nearly managed to sniff him like a puppy. "Spider?"

"Hmm?" He was staring at the screen.

"How many pillows did you own last week?"

"One."

"And how many do you own now?"

"Fucking ninety-nine or some shit."

Daisy bit her lip to keep from laughing.

She was definitely getting him a plant.

CHAPTER 8

TWO MONTHS LATER...

SPIDER LOUNGED ON THE BED, HALFWAY watching the Christmas movie that Daisy had put on but mostly watching Daisy decorate the skinny Dollar Mart Christmas tree he'd brought home the day after Thanksgiving.

"Are you going to help me with this?" She glanced over her shoulder and caught him looking at her ass. "Or are you good right there?"

"Princesa, you're asking me to give up the best view in the place." He tipped up the beer he'd grabbed from the fridge and took a long drink. "Besides, what do I know about decorating a tree?"

He'd bought the stuff for her anyway. It had been a couple of months since they started "dating," and Spider was still trying to figure out the rules. Being with Daisy wasn't like any relationship he'd known when he was growing up.

She didn't want stuff from him. Or at least she didn't want stuff that cost money. She wanted time and attention and affection. She wanted to go way faster physically than he was willing to go.

Glacier. Slow.

When he was sixteen, he'd had a "girlfriend" down south, and it was always a challenge to keep up with stuff she asked him for. She wanted a purse. She wanted a gold necklace like her friends. She wanted a new pair of shoes, and she was more than happy to give him all the blow jobs he wanted if he bought her those things.

Spider didn't judge her; it wasn't as if girls who came from the neighborhood had a lot of options. His first girlfriend didn't even go to high school; she was just trying to hustle enough that she wouldn't have to sell sex and embarrass her family.

But Daisy? She was demanding in different ways. She still hadn't let up on them being a real couple in public and all that. She wanted him to meet her parents, which was ridiculous and way too early. She shared all the things she wanted to change about the café to modernize it. She talked to him about his future and starting his own tattoo shop.

He couldn't be mad because she was so damn sweet about it, and part of Spider wanted those things too. He hadn't forgotten his talk with Bill though. He figured staying at his place with Daisy was way safer than hanging out in town and making himself a target, just in case Chino ended up being pissed at him.

He told himself over and over again: *Just another week. Just another month. Just until it's safe to breathe.*

But the end of the year was fast approaching, and Daisy was going to hear about her future soon when responses to her transfer applications started rolling in.

Eight months.

He figured he had eight months more of Daisy's sweetness, and he didn't really feel like sharing her with the rest of the world. Fuck them.

Daisy turned and swept her hand out with a flourish. "Merry Christmas, Mr. Villalobos. Your very own tree."

He set his beer on the side table and slid to the edge of the bed, standing up to walk over and put his arms around his girl. He stood behind her, arms around her waist with his chin resting on her shoulder, and swayed with the song that was playing on the TV.

"Baby, this looks so good." He kissed her neck, which she loved, and breathed in the scent of butter and cinnamon she'd carried to his place from the bakery.

Spider had bought a set of shiny red ornaments, multicolored lights, and a random mix of ornaments from a large bin that were four for a dollar. Mickey and Minnie; a bright yellow bird; a fat, red-cheeked Santa Claus. Nothing really matched, but he didn't mind. She'd made it beautiful.

Spider kissed her cheek. "When you decorate your own house someday, it's gonna be the bomb."

She squeezed his hands and knit their fingers together. "I love fixing up old things. You know those old houses south of downtown?"

"On the other side of the highway?"

"Yeah. I think they're so cool. That's where Tia Imelda lives. All the old houses have porches and all that pretty woodwork like my parents' house."

He frowned. "That whole neighborhood is way run-down. It's not like your parents' place, Daisy. There're some sketchy people over there."

"I don't think it's that bad. Imelda's never had a problem. It's always clean. And those houses have really nice yards. The new houses in town? There's nowhere to put a garden."

It didn't matter because she wasn't gonna be living in Metlin after next fall anyway. She was going away to university, and she'd probably move to a big city. She talked more about going up north instead of going down south, which was a relief.

From the television, Spider heard the beginnings of "Have Yourself a Merry Little Christmas," and he slowly turned Daisy in his arms. She slid her arms over his shoulders, and they swayed in the sparkling, colorful lights of the tree.

Eight months wasn't enough fucking time.

The thought of Daisy leaving left a sick, panicky feeling in the middle of Spider's chest. It wasn't that he expected her to stay with him, but… On the slim chance that she didn't find someone better, he could move wherever she was. He could be a tattoo artist anywhere as long as it wasn't in Southern California. Hell, maybe she'd want to get out of California permanently.

And leave her family?

He didn't think that was likely. She was loyal as hell; it was one of the things he loved about her. Like her smile and her optimism. He fucking loved that stuff.

You fucking love her.

Yeah. Yeah, he did. All the way and forever. The real kind, not the kid kind. He was old enough to know the difference now. It wasn't a surprise or a shock to his system. That feeling had been creeping up on him since the moment he saw her.

Now the certainty of loving Daisy settled into him, marking Spider as permanently as the ink under his skin.

He leaned down and captured her mouth, trying to tell her everything since he couldn't say anything. His kiss wasn't the slow, careful press of lips that he'd been keeping on a leash since their run-in at the craft store. His arms tightened around her, pressing her body into his as he kissed her over and over again, nipping at her lips and teasing his tongue along the seam of her mouth.

"Spider?"

He kissed her again.

"Spider…" Her voice was a groan and a whine. "You pick now to do this?"

His head was swimming. "What?"

She stood on her tiptoes and bit his jaw with a playful nip. "I've been trying for weeks to get you to move a little bit faster" —she poked him in the ribs— "and you pick the day I have to go to my parents' house for late Thanksgiving dinner?"

"Oh shit." He'd forgotten about that. The afternoon was gone and the sky was already dark. "How late will the dinner—?"

"Probably all night 'cause my Aunt Sunny came down with her husband and all the cousins, so they're gonna want to play a card game or something after dinner. I don't know when I'll be done." She pouted. "Sorry."

"Don't apologize. Your family is like a TV family." Spider smiled. "Seriously, princesa, it's so damn cute. Holiday dinners and card games."

"It's mostly because Imelda hates American football so much."

Spider slowly released her, quickly adjusting his jeans so she wouldn't see his erection. "You should go; I forgot about the dinner thing."

She smiled hopefully. "You could come with me."

"That would make the dinner about meeting your homeboy boyfriend and not about your aunt and her family." He kissed the tip of her nose. "It's cool."

She pressed her lips together in a pretend-scowl. "One of these days you're going to meet them, Spider."

"Maybe after the holidays, okay?" He grabbed her jacket from the corner of the bed and put it around her shoulders. "There's a lot of pressure this time of year. People get crazy."

She turned. "I didn't clean up any of the trash from decorating! It's a total mess."

"Baby, you *did* all the decorating." He laughed. "I'll clean up. Don't worry about it; you need to get going. You got a pie to get from the café, right?"

"Yes. Pumpkin, it's my aunt's favorite."

"Best fucking thing about Christmas if you ask me." He walked her to the door and down the stairs, opening her car door and giving her one long, lingering kiss that promised more.

"Tease." She pointed at him as she got in the car. "That check better not bounce later, Mr. Villalobos."

He couldn't stop the laughter. "Get out of here and be a good niece." He walked to the back fence and opened the alley gate. "I'll see you at the café tomorrow."

She backed into the alley, then waved before she pulled away.

Spider secured the gate but didn't lock it since Bill and Ruby were still out for some holiday dinner at the Elks' Club. He walked up the stairs and grabbed a garbage bag to start cleaning up the plastic packaging and the cardboard.

Someone knocked on his door, and Spider shook his head. "Daisy, how many times do I have to tell you—?" He pulled open the door and realized it wasn't Daisy returning.

It was Chino.

His old boss raised an eyebrow as he pushed his way into the apartment, looking around the sparsely furnished space. "Merry Christmas, brother."

———

DAISY WASN'T FOOLISH ENOUGH TO BRING A single pie to a Rivera-Orosco family dinner; she grabbed four. Holiday season was their busiest time of the year at Café Maya, and she and her mother always made certain to bake twice as many holiday pies as they thought they'd need.

Because pie disappeared within minutes.

"Marky, no dessert in the living room!" her mother yelled at one of her little cousins. "You eat it at the kitchen table," she snapped at him, and Mark abruptly changed course, rolling his eyes behind Tia Alicia's back as he dragged his feet away from the television playing a Christmas movie and the lively card game that had already started in the den.

"My baby." Her mom put an arm around Daisy's shoulders and drew her close. "This might be your last Thanksgiving at home for a while."

"What?" Daisy blinked. "Why would you say that?"

"Oh, I don't know," her mother said. "You're going away to school next fall. You may want to spend Thanksgiving with friends or be too busy to come home." A smile crept at the corner of her mouth. "Who knows?

You might meet a nice boy at the university. Another student, you know? If he wants you to spend the holidays with him—"

"I will say no." Daisy felt embarrassed even contemplating it. "Because I spend the holidays with my family." And she was in love with Spider; she just didn't know how to tell him, much less her parents, who didn't even know the man existed.

Spider would never ask her to skip the holidays with her family, and he only knew them by reputation. It felt physically painful to imagine him alone on Christmas. Thanksgiving had been bad enough even though he appreciated the plate of turkey, cornbread, and apple salad she'd brought him.

"I'm just saying that when you're independent, things will change," her mother said. "And that's fine, mija! That's normal. Your dad and I don't expect you to always be here, you know? You need to get out. Meet new people. Experience the world more." Alicia gripped her shoulder. "We are so *proud* of you, Daisy."

"I didn't turn in any of my applications for the fall." Daisy blurted it so loudly that every eye in the room swung toward her. "I filled them out." Her heart was pounding. "But I didn't send them in."

Roberto stood from the card table with a scowl. "Why not?"

Daisy looked around the room in panic, wishing she'd convinced Spider to come with her. This was not what she'd planned, but the thought of leaving Metlin, of not being here for Thanksgivings and Christmases, of missing Tia Imelda and the rest of her family...

She'd panicked! She didn't want to spend holidays with strangers.

"I don't want to go away to college." She blinked rapidly. "I've tried to tell you so many times. I don't even want to go to a big college." She caught her aunt's gaze; the old woman was smiling at her and nodding softly. "Maybe I'll take some business classes or management or something in Fresno, but I want to stay here. I want to take over the café and make it mine." She looked at her father. "I don't want to leave Metlin. I never did." She looked at her mother. "And I'm dating someone here in town. We've been together for a couple of months now, and I love him."

If her declaration of *non*-independence had rendered the room silent, her declaration of love made it explode.

CHAPTER 9

"SO, LITTLE BROTHER—"

"I'm not your little brother." Spider looked at the card table, no longer covered by the pretty red cloth that Daisy had brought over. He'd tucked it away when Chino brought out his cigarettes and asked to smoke.

Chino chuckled. "You're not very little anymore, are you? Skinny kid got *ripped*, eh?"

Spider tapped his thumb on the card table. "Exercise keeps me focused."

"You still doing ink?"

Spider shrugged. "That's all I do, man. That's all I know."

"How'd you find your way up here?" Chino took a long drag and reached for the glass Daisy had been drinking out of earlier. "Here." He tapped the edge of the ash into the glass. "Don't want to mess up your place, huh?"

"Appreciate it." Spider sat with his legs spread and his chair angled away from the table, his left hand on the table and his right loose and ready on his thigh. He couldn't take his eyes off the black ash swirling in the bottom of Daisy's glass.

Dirty.

Chino took another draw on his cigarette. "You left in a hurry, man."

"My mom got killed because they were trying to get me. It seemed like a good idea to leave fast."

Chino nodded, his curly hair falling over his forehead and softening the hard expression in his eyes. "I get that, *ese*, but we waited for you to come back when shit died down. It never happened."

Spider looked directly at Chino. "I got my mom killed."

"So that's it?" He looked offended. "It wasn't us that killed her, man. We shut that shit down after you—"

"I'm not blaming you." Spider lifted a finger on his right hand. "I never blamed you for that, Chino. I blamed myself. I'm the one that brought that on her, not you."

Chino let out a slow stream of smoke and nodded thoughtfully. "I appreciate that. You know our crew ain't never gone after moms like that. That's bullshit the Marav—"

"I'm not in the middle of anyone's feud anymore, Chino. I'm clean. I don't touch anything that might come back on you; I do not fucking talk to cops. I keep my shit close, you know what I mean?"

Chino narrowed his eyes. "No one ever called you a snitch, Spider."

"So why did you come looking for me?"

"Why'd you stay up in fuckin' nowhere without calling us once?"

Spider nodded. "That's fair." He lit a cigarette to keep his hands from shaking. "At first I stayed up here 'cause this is where I ran out of money." He was couching it for Chino because that wasn't the real reason. "And then, when I had some cash, I was working for an old couple who needed the help out on their farm. They'd been good to me, you know? Didn't want to just take off."

Chino nodded. "I can appreciate that."

"After a while, I met the guy who owns the local studio. He liked my stuff and I started working for him." He took another drag on his cigarette. "I'm not... in that life anymore. I'm out."

Chino smiled. "But Spider, you're still part of my crew. You know that, man."

Spider's heart sank, and a chill ran through him.

"When my boys join my family, they're *family*." Chino's hand landed on his. "Family, Spider." The man looked at the Christmas tree. "You got a good thing here, but this is crazy, bro. People still talk about your work all over the city. No one's as good as you were."

Fuck no, they aren't. He didn't say it. Bravado didn't work on Chino; he only wanted submission.

"That's very flattering. Thank you."

"Flattering, eh?" Chino grinned. "Damn, you got all respectable on us, Spider."

Spider kept his eyes on the table.

Chino leaned toward him, "Brother, I don't want you to come back and be a soldier." He snorted. "I got enough guys for that. I'm not gonna waste your damn hands on a gun."

Spider looked up. Chino didn't want him back?

"I want you to come back and do what you're doing here!" He glanced at the neat stack of notebooks by Spider's bedside table. "Just better."

"I don't—"

"You're living in a shitty little apartment over a garage, homes. You're working for someone else. When you come back, we get you your own house. Get you a sweet place in Boyle Heights. We set you up with your own place where you run the show. You got, like, three colleges within miles of that neighborhood. You'd make *bank*, Spider. Then you could get a kid or two under you that you can train up."

Spider kept his eyes on Chino, looking for any signs of dishonesty, but he couldn't see them. Chino was actually offering to set Spider up in his own place with a house, a business—

"We'd be your *investors*," Chino continued. "You could keep most of the money—we'd only take a cut— and you give your brothers the family discount." Chino shrugged. "Keep it in the family. I got *big* plans for you, man."

His gut and his head were battling. His gut told him that Chino was trying to pull something; his head was filled with the idea of his own house. His own place. The rush of celebration, of everyone eager to get his needle on their skin.

It would take him years to build up anything close to an independent clientele in Metlin, and it's not like people had as much money here as they did in LA. He could charge twice or three times as much tattooing customers down south, which would more than offset the discount he'd be obligated to give Chino's crew.

A bank in Metlin would never lend him money. But the gangs? Well, if there was one thing you could say for organized crime: they invested in their own.

He watched Chino pull the cigarette from his mouth, his inked fingers deftly ashing into Daisy's glass.

Daisy.

He felt her slipping away.

She would never be okay with this. She came from good people. Regular people.

You did too, once upon a time.

He loved Daisy, but he only had her for another eight months. She'd be going away, and then where would he be? Stuck in Metlin, seeing her around town on summer breaks and holidays. Watching when she brought a normal boyfriend into the café to meet her aunt and her mom. Loving her like a pathetic asshole while she moved on with her life.

There was no way Daisy would ever go down south and no way that he would want her to. Even if she was okay with him being associated with Chino's crew—which she wouldn't fucking be—it would put her in harm's way, just like his mom.

"Spider." Chino's hand landed on his forearm, right over the two letters that had sealed his fate at age thirteen. "It's time to come home."

"Chino" —he tapped his lighter on the table, his mind spinning— "this is a really good deal, man, but I gotta—"

"There's no rush." Chino raised a hand. "Spend Christmas with your girl." The man smiled, and a glint of gold reflected in the lights from the Christmas tree. "She looks *sweet*." He slid a card out of his wallet and tapped the edge on the table before he laid it down. "But this isn't where you belong, Spider. You and I both know it." He stood and dropped his cigarette butt in Daisy's glass. "My number's on the card if you want to talk, but I'll be back in a couple of weeks." He drew Spider into a hard, backslapping hug. "I missed you, man. It's gonna be good to have you back."

Daisy had managed to stop crying by the time she got to Spider's door, but she knew her eyes were red and swollen. There was no avoiding it.

There had been so much yelling.

She was the good kid. Her parents had never yelled at her like that before. She did her homework and cleaned her room. She helped around the house, and usually the extent of her mother's anger was a pair of rolled eyes when Alicia had to remind Daisy twice to empty the dishwasher.

Nothing had prepared her for that blowup.

Her father had yelled at her. Her mother had burst into tears. Her aunts all asked if she was pregnant.

Seriously! What was that?

Kiko and all her cousins had fled, knowing that the barest hint of defiance or rebellion could turn the blast of familial fury their direction. She couldn't fault their survival instincts. She'd done the same thing herself. When that many Riveras, Oroscos, Mendels, and Rojases were yelling, you headed for the nearest exit.

They were disappointed in her.

She was ungrateful.

She was throwing away her future.

Daisy knocked on Spider's door, confused when it took him so long to respond. His car was in his parking spot, but he did like to walk; maybe he was out.

She knocked again. "Spider?" The door swung open and the smell of cigarette smoke made her nose twitch. "Hey."

"What are you doing here?"

Daisy looked up, blinking her swollen eyes. "I told my parents."

He went utterly still. "Told your parents what?"

She was so tired. All she wanted was to snuggle into Spider's pile of pillows and have her secret boyfriend—who wasn't exactly a secret anymore—cuddle her. "Can I come in?"

He nearly jerked her arm, pulling her into the house. "What did you tell them?"

She looked around and tried to think through her exhaustion and head fog. "You were smoking inside?"

Spider smoked, but he was fastidious and he didn't like ashes on his floor or smoke in his clothes. She'd never even seen him smoke inside.

Daisy turned and looked at him. "What's going on?"

For the first time since she'd known him, she couldn't read his face. He was wearing a mask she didn't recognize.

"Nothing." He cleared his throat and walked over, putting his arms around her. "Tell me what happened with your parents."

She put her head on his chest and her arms around his waist, glad that he sounded more normal. "I told them I didn't turn in the transfer applications. And that I wanted to stay in Metlin and I didn't want to go to school anymore; I want to run the café."

His arms tightened around her. "You didn't turn in the applications?"

She sighed. "Don't you get mad at me too."

"I asked you, like, two weeks ago, and you told me you'd finished them."

"I did finish them. I just didn't…" Daisy's eyes fell on a black duffel bag sitting by the closet. She lifted her head and frowned. "What is that?"

"What's what?" Spider's head followed hers. "Um… I was cleaning out my closet."

"Why?"

Spider hardly owned any clothes. Daisy had seen him wear three different shirts and three different pairs of jeans, all meticulously folded. He had two white T-shirts and two black ones. And he needed to clean out his closet?

She took a step back. She hadn't been looking when she came in, but there was something different about the room. "Spider, what's going on?"

She saw the trash neatly bagged by the door. The dishes were washed and dried on the shelf. The TV was off and the bed was made. One pillow was sitting on the edge, clearly placed there next to Spider's black canvas jacket.

She looked and saw that the gold medallion that had hung on the wall next to the sink was gone, along with the prayer card of Saint Luke.

Her heart began to race. "You're leaving."

Daisy looked at Spider, and he didn't deny it.

He didn't deny it.

I left LA in twenty minutes, princesa. I could probably do it in half the time now.

She turned in a circle, feeling like her world had tilted sideways. "You're leaving Metlin."

"Daisy—"

"Don't!" She felt her heart crack in half, and she raised her hand, putting whatever barrier she could between them. "Don't lie to me."

He swallowed hard, and the mask he'd been wearing slipped. "Will you sit down?" He pulled out a chair at the card table. "Daisy, please."

"I don't want to sit down," she whispered.

Maybe it was a dream. Maybe it was all a dream. If she sat—if she touched anything and she didn't wake up —then it would be real.

"Baby, please." His eyes were shining. "Please sit down."

CHAPTER 10

NO ONE HAD TOLD Spider that it physically hurt to see someone you love crying. That was fucking important information if you asked him. School taught him fucking algebra, but they didn't teach him that?

And that's why school was bullshit.

Daisy was sitting across from him, one hand in both of his and the other clenched so tight on her lap that he could see her knuckles were white.

"Chino found me," he said softly. "That's my old boss. The guy who ran the crew I was in down south."

Daisy's eyes were wide. "Did he try to hurt you?"

"No." Spider huffed out a breath and looked at the scarred table. "He wanted to... invest in me."

"What?" She sounded confused.

"He wants me to move down south, open up a shop and all that. Give them a cut of the profits and do ink for his crew for cheap." Spider couldn't look at her, but he could imagine her face. She would be horrified. Repulsed. Disgusted probably.

"I guess that's a pretty good offer."

Spider's head jerked up. She hadn't sounded disgusted; she sounded sad.

"I'm not going!"

She looked at the duffel bag. "It looks like you are to me."

Her face, which was normally so glowing, looked pale and tired. It was as if the bright, beautiful thing that made her Daisy had drained away; the sight made Spider even sicker.

"I'm not going with Chino," he said. "I can't lie; I thought about it. For a few minutes I considered it. I'd have my own shop. They said they'd get me my own house and everything." One hand rubbed the back of her neck. "Not all their businesses are drugs, you know? There are some that are just kind of..."

"Criminally adjacent?" She looked at him. "Illegal-ish?"

"Yeah. But for the first time ever, I'd be my own boss."

She stared at a spot on the wall. "Except you wouldn't be. Not really."

Yeah, she was a smart one. She caught on quick.

"Exactly." Spider nodded. "I wouldn't be dealing, but if they had a shipment of stuff they needed to hide? They wouldn't think twice about leaving it at my house.

I'd always be afraid of the cops; I'd always be worried they were looking at me for something."

"No one would want to live that way."

"But a lot of people do," Spider said. "When I was thirteen, that was normal."

Daisy finally looked at him. "Thirteen?"

If he was leaving, she deserved the truth. "I got jumped into Chino's crew when I was young. When I was real little, my parents taught us to avoid those kids, you know? It wasn't all gangs and shit. A lot of straight people lived in the neighborhood too. Regular people."

"Like your parents."

"Yeah." He swallowed the lump in his throat. "I promised my dad, but I only made it a few months after he died." He ran his thumb over her knuckles. "I was... pissed. Angry at the world. And my mom was working out of the house, cleaning big fancy places and then getting half the money she was supposed to get."

"Why?" Daisy asked. "People just stole from her?"

"She was legal but she was a widow, didn't speak much English. She used to..." Spider coughed and blinked hard. "I was embarrassed by her. After my dad died and she had to work cleaning houses, I thought... she was embarrassing."

Daisy squeezed his hand. "You were thirteen. Every kid thinks his mom is embarrassing when they're thirteen."

"I went looking for them, you know? Chino's crew. I knew who they were, and some of the kids in his gang

who were just a little older than me? They had *money*. I
would see them with a couple hundred bucks sometimes. Which to me at the time? Oh my God, princesa,
that was like a fortune."

"You wanted to have money. That's normal, Spider."

"I was Manuel then." He smiled at the memory of his
father saying his name. "I was named after my grandfather. Sometimes my dad called me Manito."

"Did the gang...? Did they make you change your
name?"

"No." He'd been the one to change it; he'd been the
one to kill that part of himself. "I didn't want... My
mother called me Manuel. I didn't want Chino calling
me the same thing."

She had both his hands in hers now. "That makes
sense. Also, you have a giant spider tattooed on your
head."

"I got that when I was fifteen." Spider looked up.
"But the name came first. I thought it was funny, you
know? I had a book about spiders when I was a kid, one
of those picture books. And I remember reading how
spiders were the helpers of the animal kingdom. They
ate bugs and shit. But, like, everyone is scared of them
even though most of them aren't poisonous. They're
these nice, shy bugs that everyone thinks are killers."

"But they really aren't dangerous at all." Daisy's eyes
were shining. "What made you leave LA?"

He'd talked around it before, but he'd never admitted
the truth to her. "My mom got killed by a bullet meant

for me. She died because these guys were coming after Chino's crew. Everyone, even their little shit of a tattoo artist." He blinked. "My mom died because of me."

The truth landed between them with a silent thud. Spider took a deep breath and tried to think through the pain.

Losing his dad.

Losing his mother.

Losing Daisy.

Life had taken his dad from him, but the other two were on him. He never should have risked his mother's life by joining Chino's crew. He never should have allowed himself to get close to Daisy when he knew what kind of past he had.

"Spider." Daisy's voice broke through his self-loathing. "I don't want you to go down south."

"I'm not going to." He leaned toward her. "But that's why I have to leave Metlin. Chino knows I'm here. He told me tonight that I'm still in his crew, that we're family. He kept saying it over and over again, calling me brother, talking about my future. He left for now, but he'll be back."

"You don't have any future with him."

He squeezed her hands. "I know that. I promise I do. I'm not going back, but I can't stay here."

Her breath hitched. "Why not?"

"Because he'll come after me," Spider whispered. "He's playing nice right now, playing the forgiving big brother. But when he looks at me, he sees money, and he's not gonna forget about that. That's profit out of his pocket."

"Can you go to the co—?"

He put a finger on her lips. "Don't even finish saying that. I'll be dead, Daisy. I'll just be dead if I do that."

She looked around his spare apartment, at the duffel bag and the spot where his prayer card used to be. At the precious little Christmas tree she'd set up. It was the one time Spider had ever wished he owned a camera. He wanted a fucking picture of that tree before he left.

I love you so fucking much.

He wanted to tell her, but he shouldn't. That would be a shitty thing to do when he'd just told her he was leaving.

"You can't stay here tonight." Spider stood and held his hand out. "Let me take you to Betsy's. I know you had a fight with your folks and you don't want to go home, but I don't know if any of Chino's guys are still around. It's not safe here. Let me take you to the bookshop."

She was silent, but she nodded and stood.

"Emmie's mom, Yvonne, is gone for the next couple of weeks to Vegas, playing at this club with her band, so her room will be empty." He grabbed her keys and ushered her toward the door.

She stopped before they walked out and turned toward him. "Are you going to leave once you drop me at Betsy's place?"

He paused to think. Chino had said he could take a

couple of weeks. Maybe it would be better to make sure Daisy was settled, make sure she was okay with her folks before he left. After all, with him out of Metlin, she'd probably want to go to college, right? And that was the best option. That's what she should do.

"If you say you're leaving," she said quietly, "I'm not going to Betsy's."

Fuck, she could be stubborn when she put her mind to it. Pretty and happy and easygoing most of the time, but when the woman dug her heels in, she wasn't going to move.

"I'll stay for a week," he said. "That's all I can promise."

———

BETSY DIDN'T ASK ANY QUESTIONS WHEN THEY showed up at her house at midnight. She took one look at Daisy and nearly shoved them inside before putting a kettle on for tea, making Daisy drink a cup of chamomile while she changed the sheets in her daughter's room.

Spider tried to help, but Betsy forced him to sit at the kitchen table and keep an eye on Daisy, which was its own kind of torture.

She wouldn't look at him, not that he could blame her. He hadn't exactly made her promises, but he hadn't interrupted her when she dreamed about his future. She'd talked about working at the café and seeing him more when she was finished with school. She talked about him opening his own place, and he didn't tell her it could never happen.

For a little while, a few precious weeks, he'd started to think her vision for the future was possible. Maybe. Just a little bit.

She was asleep the moment her head hit the pillow in Yvonne's room.

Betsy closed the door and ushered him downstairs to talk on the old worn couch in a corner of the bookshop. "What's going on?"

"She had a big fight with her parents." He stared at a shelf full of biographies. "Told them she didn't want to go away to school." Martin Luther King. *The Autobiography of Malcom X.* Theodore Roosevelt. Catherine the Great. They probably had bigger problems than him, and they'd made it into the history books and all that shit.

Of course, they were all dead too.

Betsy wasn't a fool. "A fight with her parents is not what put that look in Daisy's eyes."

Spider pressed his lips together.

"She's in love with you," Betsy said. "Did you two think Imelda and I didn't know you were together? You think you're very silent and mysterious, but I've known you for five years. You're in—"

"Don't." He leaned forward, bracing his elbows on his knees. "They found me, Betsy."

She sat up and leaned forward. "The gang?"

"Chino. I'm guessing he must have figured out my real name after I took off. Probably went through my mom's place after the shooting. Then when I got my tattoo license—"

"You have to put your legal name and an address down for that," Betsy said. "With the state board. That's how they found you."

"Yeah." He didn't know the exact details, but she'd guessed the same things Spider had. "I was getting ready to leave when Daisy came over."

"Spider." Her voice was soft and reproachful. "Were you going to leave without telling her?"

"I don't know." He groaned. "Betsy, I don't know what the hell I'm doing. I thought three hundred miles would be enough to keep them away, you know? It's been five years. I'm not doing any shit that would put me on their radar, but Chino tracked me down and wants to give me money to start my own place or something."

"You're not considering that, are you?" Betsy frowned. "Spider, you said you'd never go back. Your life would be controlled by them. I don't care what they tell you, they are not going to allow you to—"

"I'm not going to do it," he said. "I told you years ago: I don't make the same mistake twice."

Except Daisy. Daisy had been a mistake. Of course, there was only one Daisy, so how the hell was he supposed to have seen her coming?

"What do you want to do?" Betsy asked.

"What I have to do. I'm going to run. Again."

And again.

And again.

And again, until the memory of the dumb kid named Spider who was pretty good at tattooing disappeared from everyone's mind. Hopefully he wouldn't be an old man before that happened.

"Spider, that's not a solution. You can't live like this," Betsy said. "You're never going to have a future if you keep running. You're always going to be looking over your shoulder."

"Tell me what the hell I'm supposed to do then?" He looked at her. "You're the smartest person I know, Betsy. Tell me what I should do that will keep Daisy safe. And you and Emmie. And Bill and Ruby. Hell, this whole town has been good to me. More than a skinny gangbanger deserved—don't even try to argue. And now the one thing I can do to return the favor and keep everyone safe is leave."

"And break Daisy's heart."

Spider felt his chest ache. "I don't want to do it, Betsy, I just don't see any other way. If I'm wrong" —he reached over and squeezed her hand— "tell me how."

CHAPTER 11

DAISY WOKE UP BEFORE DAWN, having slept fitfully through the night. She'd had dreams of a car accident and felt jolted and sore. There were taillights disappearing and a sudden vacuum of cold that sucked the breath from her body.

She got up, used the bathroom, and then returned to bed, hiding under the covers to escape the cold in the old brick building with wooden floors.

"Daisy?" Emmie whispered outside the door. "Are you awake?"

"Yeah." Daisy kept her voice low. "You can come in if you want."

The door creaked open, and Emmie slipped inside the bedroom, her pale blue sweatpants nearly the same color as the light peeking through the window.

"Hey." The girl looked flustered. "I heard you last night, but I didn't want to get in trouble. Are you okay?"

That was a good question. Was she okay? In a sense, yes. She was fine. She was physically well, had options for her future, and eventually her parents would calm down. No doubt they thought she was shacking up with her "secret boyfriend," but they wouldn't think she was homeless or anything.

"I'm okay." She checked her cell phone, and there was one call from her mother and another from Kiko. "Give me a second, Em." She called Kiko back and waited for him to pick up, knowing that it might go to voice mail before he answered. Her little brother was a sound sleeper and it was early.

"Yeah?"

"Hey, Kiko, it's me."

"Are you okay?" He cleared his throat. "Mom and Dad waited up last night, but you didn't come home. You're at your boyfriend's, right? Or Olivia's place?"

She hadn't even thought about her cousin, though that was definitely an option. "I'm at Betsy's place. Emmie's mom is gone right now, so I spent the night here."

"At the bookstore?"

"Yeah." She sat up. "Just tell everyone I'm fine, okay? I don't really want to talk to Mom or Dad right now."

"Yeah, okay."

"Were they more pissed about the school thing or the boyfriend?"

Across the room, Emmie's eyes went wide.

Kiko answered, "Definitely the school thing. And the fact that you didn't tell them sooner."

"Dude, I've been trying to tell them for, like, a year now."

"Don't get mad at me; I wasn't surprised." Kiko yawned. "But seriously, who are you dating? Why's it some big secret? He's not married or anything, is he?"

"Ew! Kiko, what the heck? I would never—"

"So why the big secret? You're twenty; they know you've dated before."

"It's Spider, and it wasn't that I didn't want to tell them, it's that *he* thought Mom and Dad wouldn't approve of him."

Emmie slid off the chair where she'd been perched and did a ridiculous wiggle dance that made Daisy want to laugh. And maybe cry a little.

Kiko was quiet. "Spider, the guy who works at Bill and Ruby's tattoo place?"

"Yeah." For how much longer, she had no idea.

"He seems cool and he's really quiet. That's totally not who I was expecting."

"He's very private." She frowned. "Wait, who were you expecting?"

"But Lazy Daze, that's messed up. What? He's, like, embarrassed by you or something?"

"I told you…" She sighed. "It's complicated, and I should go. If anyone asks, I'm at Betsy's. Tell Tia Imelda I'm here; I don't want her to worry."

"I'll tell them." Kiko laughed. "I just thought of something funny."

"What?"

"I'll tell you later. It kind of takes some explaining." Without another word, her brother hung up the phone and Daisy could turn her attention to Emmie, who was still awkwardly dancing around the room.

"Really?"

"I knew it!" Emmie whisper-shouted. "I knew he was in love with you! Ever since the time when you came into the bookstore."

Spider? In love? Her heart flipped over; then it twisted in her chest and it felt like the worst case of heartburn ever. "That's ridiculous. We'd just met. He'd barely said two words to me before that day."

"So?" Emmie shrugged. "Elizabeth and Mr. Darcy only saw each other, like, four or five times before he fell in love with her. Spider sees you, like, every day."

"To get coffee."

"Yeah. You ever wonder why a guy who only has four T-shirts and three pairs of jeans spent the money to buy coffee every day?"

Daisy swallowed hard. "Emmie, I know it may seem romantic, but it takes more than—"

"I'm just saying that he loves you. It's totally obvious, and I've known Spider longer than you, so I would know." Emmie looked at her from the corner of her eye. "Do you not love him?"

Duh. "Loving Spider is not the problem."

115

"Does he know that?"

"What?" Daisy rubbed her eyes and pulled her tangled hair into a messy bun. "That there's a problem? Yeah. I mean, he's pretty much the one—"

"No, that you love him." Emmie leaned on the edge of her mother's dressing table. "Because you should tell him that." The girl's eyes turned inward. "I don't think many people have told him that in his life."

Emmie's words hit Daisy straight in the chest. "You really love him a lot, don't you?"

Emmie smiled, then wrinkled her nose. "Not like that though. He's like... I don't know. If I had a brother, I kind of imagine he would be like Spider."

"Yeah."

Emmie kicked her foot out and pointed her toe. "I had this superweird dream once that I was getting married—not to Spider, that would be gross—but he was there." Her cheeks turned a little red. "He was walking me down the aisle. Like, to give me away. Weird, right?"

"Not weird." Daisy couldn't even imagine being an only child. But Emmie was. So was Spider. "Hey, Em?"

"Yeah?"

"I'm going to get dressed and go over to his house real quick." Daisy was already getting out of bed. "Tell Betsy where I went, okay?"

"Sure." Emmie smiled. "You're gonna tell him, aren't you?"

"Mind your business." Daisy couldn't bring herself to

smile—her heart was still bruised—but she was starting to have an idea.

Spider belonged in Metlin. It would hurt Daisy's heart to see him leave, but it would shatter Emmie. It would leave Betsy on her own. And she was pretty sure Spider would be miserable.

This wasn't just about him and her. This was bigger.

———

She knocked on his door and he answered, still wearing the black T-shirt he'd been wearing the night before. His eyes were red, and it looked like he hadn't gotten a bit of sleep.

Spider pulled her inside and quickly shut the door.

"No one is outside," she said. "I looked when I turned on the street. I know all the cars here, and no one—"

She stopped talking because he kissed her.

Spider kissed her over and over, like a man starving for her lips. He cupped her cheek with one palm as his arm came around the small of her back and he pressed their bodies together.

His kiss felt sweet and desperate at the same time.

"Spider?" She pulled away and gasped for breath. "Did something else happen?"

"I love you." He kept his eyes closed and pressed his forehead to hers. "I wasn't going to tell you, but I already fucking lied to you enough, and not telling you feels like a lie." His fingers dug into the muscle at her back. "I fucking love you, and I don't care if you don't love me. It's okay if you don't, you know? But it wasn't right—"

"I love you too."

His eyebrows furrowed and his grip turned tighter. "Princesa, I don't know what to do. I just… I need someone to tell me what to do."

"You can't leave." She leaned back and forced him to look at her. "That's the one thing I know: you need to stay in Metlin. Not just for me. I mean, I could go with you. But Emmie and Betsy can't. Neither can Bill or—"

"What?" He blinked as if the idea had never occurred to him. "You go with *me*?"

"You think I was angry about your leaving?" Daisy asked. "I mean, yeah, I was. But I was madder you weren't planning to tell me, and I was extra hurt that you weren't going to ask me to come with you."

"Your family is here," he said. "Less than twenty-four hours ago, you had a huge fight with them because you didn't want to leave Metlin."

"I don't, but I don't want to lose you." Daisy laid her head on Spider's shoulder. "When I'm with you, I feel peaceful and safe. Yes, obviously I think you're superhot, but that's not why I'm with you."

"You think I'm superhot?"

"Shut *up*."

He chuckled, and it was the best thing she'd heard in days.

"You know you're sexy," Daisy said. "Don't pretend."

"You're the one who's sexy." Spider's voice was low and growly in a way that made Daisy's insides jump. His mask was completely gone, and the strict control he usually exercised seemed to have been forgotten.

He held her in a loose embrace, his fingers trailing along her neck, behind her ear, and along her collarbone as the hand at the small of her back dipped lower, stroking over the curve of her butt and teasing the sensitive skin there.

"So fucking sexy."

She pressed her mouth to his neck. "Spider."

"Tell me to stop." Spider pressed kisses along her collarbone. "If you don't want to—"

"I want to." She felt a near desperate need for him, as though if she let go of him, he might disappear. "Please."

"I love you." He kissed her hard. "I fucking love you so much, and I've never done this before."

She frowned and leaned back. "What? You've never—"

"Not like making love." He drew her over to the bed and flipped on the small space heater he hardly ever used. Then he reached down and slipped off her shoes. "You're so fucking sweet, and I just want… Maybe we shouldn't—"

"Take off your shirt." Her voice was quiet but firm.

If she gave Spider too much time to think about this, he'd manage to talk himself out of sex for some noble and completely unnecessary reason. She'd been wanting to sleep with him for weeks. Okay, months. She could admit that she wanted to jump his bones when he was barely more than a stranger at the café who liked his coffee black with three sugars.

"Daisy." He pulled off his T-shirt in a lithe, sexy move she'd only seen on TV. Then he lifted her shirt and pressed a line of kisses along her stomach, swirling his tongue in circles around her belly button and softly biting at the skin underneath.

"Keep your shirt on right now." Spider looked up from the edge of the bed. "It's cold."

Was it? Daisy already felt like she was going to come out of her skin. "Okay."

He slowly drew her leg up, propped her foot on the edge of the bed, and ran his cheek along the inside of her thigh. "Do you like this?"

She felt her face burning. "I don't know. I've never... I mean—"

"Fuck, you're gonna be sweet." He leaned forward and bit her belly again, using deft fingers to unbutton and unzip her pants. He eased them down her body, then played with the edge of her panties, a smile flirting around the corners of his mouth. "Your underwear has tiny pictures of cookies on them."

"Yes." She refused to be embarrassed. Some people had sexy underwear; hers could only be classified as cute. She was fine with that. "I am a baker, and my cookies have won awards."

"Really?"

"Yes at the county fair when I was in eighth grade. I got first place."

"You are so fucking cute." He looked up, his eyes on her as he slid his hands under her panties, cupping her butt with wide, warm hands and making her gasp. "Yeah, I think you're gonna like this, princesa."

She looked at the top of his dark head and watched his tattooed shoulders flex as he worked her panties down her legs. The air pricked her skin, but she barely noticed.

"It used to make me mad when you called me princesa," Daisy said.

"Oh yeah?"

"But then I imagined that I was wearing a crown and you were kneeling in front of me, doing this exact thing, and so I didn't mind it after that."

He looked up and his lips were flushed. He licked them, and his eyes met hers. "I am getting you a fucking tiara for Christmas."

His hands lifted her body to his mouth, and then Daisy couldn't even think.

It was... strange at first, but then it wasn't. Oh God, it *wasn't*. It was almost too much sensation as Spider tasted, lapped, sucked, and generally made Daisy his own personal dessert.

At one point she actually stumbled, and Spider pulled his mouth away, stood, lifted her, and then dropped her right back on the bed in a move so swift she hardly registered what had happened until she was staring at the popcorn ceiling.

Daisy'd had an orgasm before because she really did need to understand what all the fuss was about, but it was nothing compared to being at Spider's mercy.

Her climax came so suddenly she bowed up out of bed, shouting his name, but he didn't let go. She finally had to push him away, and he still kept his mouth on her, kissing along the inside of her thigh, then up over her hip, along the sensitive skin of her belly.

Daisy was fairly sure that whatever nerve endings she'd previously owned had been tripled. She was hot and cold at the same time. Her legs were sore, and she felt like she'd been doing sit-ups, her abdominal muscles were so tense.

Spider kissed up her torso, his hands pushing up her T-shirt and baring her bra. "This has to go." He reached behind her and unsnapped it before he dragged her up to sitting, pulled her T-shirt and bra off, and tossed them on the floor.

Then he sat up on his heels and stared. "You're the prettiest fucking woman I've ever seen in my entire life."

Daisy hadn't been feeling self-conscious until that moment. Something about Spider's open appraisal had her shifting on the bed.

He frowned. "Are you cold?"

Sure, that was a good excuse. "A little."

He eased the blankets from beneath her and then covered her up before he walked to the bookcase and opened a book. He grabbed a foil-wrapped condom from the inside, then put it back while Daisy admired the line of muscle that ran along the side of his abdominals and the tight curve of his butt.

He turned and saw her watching. "You like how I look?"

"Yes. What book was that?"

Spider smiled. *"North American Birdwatching."*

"Oh, that's nice." She was trying to be cool, but seeing so much of Spider's skin was starting to break her. She wanted to touch all of it. From the swirling flourishes that framed his neck to the roman numerals on his shoulders, the Aztec circle on his elbow, and the flames on his forearm.

And that was only one arm. His entire body was a work of art.

"You're so handsome." She sat up, holding the covers to her chest as she scooted over to make room for him on the narrow bed.

"Princesa…," he murmured. "If you think I'm okay to look at, then that's all I give a shit about." He shoved down his jeans and boxers, and then slid into bed before she could look at him for too long.

They were under the covers, skin to skin, and Daisy felt like she was about to explode. "So, um, I've never… I mean, I've had sex, but I never was able to come just from that."

He took her mouth in a long, luscious kiss that stole the last thoughts from her mind. "Yeah, that's not a big deal. A lot of girls can't come that way." He reached down and put on the condom. "That's why ladies always come first." The corner of his mouth turned up. "Plus that really fucking turns me on. Please tell me you like it."

She nodded, but that was all she could manage before he was kissing her again, working his way down her body until he got to her breasts, which he also seemed to be very excited about.

Daisy had never come from just sex, but she decided Spider might just be able to change that. She stopped trying to predict what he was going to do, held on to his shoulders, and let him do whatever he wanted to her body because it all felt incredibly good.

When he finally slid inside her, she'd come twice from his hands and his mouth. She decided she might need glasses because she could no longer see straight, and then Spider was in her, his eyes locked on her face, and everything came into focus.

She would love this man for the rest of her life.

She would do anything for him. Fight any battle. Climb over every obstacle.

Spider was hers.

And she was never letting him go.

CHAPTER 12

SPIDER WAS STARING at the duffel bag again.

Give me time.

It had already been six days since Chino had found him. Daisy had asked him for time, but the itch to pack his shit and run was nearly overwhelming. It was Friday afternoon, and Spider wasn't working. A week ago, he would have called Daisy and told her to come over after the café closed at three. He liked watching her when she talked about her day, liked to watch her face when she told stories.

Everything about Daisy was animated. She talked with her hands, she imitated voices, and she laughed so damn much.

It was a weird and humbling feeling to love someone who was such a good person.

She loves you too.

Spider wanted to believe it, but like it had been with Betsy, it was taking time to sink in.

The duffel bag stared at him, a black eye narrowed and watching him from the corner by his closet. His grandmother's medallion sat in a small dish in the center of the card table, and underneath it was the card that the priest at Saint Mark's had given him when he'd caught Spider sketching on the program before mass.

Someone knocked at the door, and Spider nearly jumped to his feet. He walked on cat feet to the narrow kitchen window and peeked out. Daisy would have announced herself; so would Bill. He wasn't expecting company, and Chino's visit had shaken him.

He saw a Mexican man of medium build with a full head of silver-black hair and a collared plaid shirt. The man was wearing worn jeans and work boots that were a long way from new.

Whoever he was, he didn't look like he knew Chino.

Maybe he was a friend of Mr. Juarez's, the rancher Spider had worked for. He wondered if Mr. and Mrs. Juarez were okay.

With that thought at the back of his mind, Spider opened the door a crack. "Can I help you?"

"Are you Spider?" the man asked.

"Who's asking?"

"My name is Roberto Rivera; I'm Daisy's father."

Oh shit. That might be worse than Chino.

Spider's heart began to race, but he opened the door and motioned for Mr. Rivera to enter. He was glad he wasn't a slob, but there were three cups in the sink he'd been putting off, and there was no subtle way he could clean them before Daisy's dad noticed.

The older man was scanning the apartment like a cop. He looked at the duffel bag by the door, the neatly made bed, the television and the kitchen.

"Would you like to sit down?" Spider asked. "I don't have anything to drink. I can get you water or milk, but that's all."

"I don't need a drink." The man's hands hung in his pockets, but he removed them when he sat and crossed his arms over his chest. "So you're working for Bill and Ruby?"

For now. "Yes, sir."

"As an artist? Do you have a... a license?" He frowned. "I don't understand tattoos, but I'm assuming there's a license of some kind."

Spider sat across from him. "I completed the state-approved course for Bloodborne Pathogen Exposure Control, and I've been tattooing since I was about fourteen. I've been an artist for as long as I can remember."

Mr. Rivera's eyes never moved from him. "No one legal would have let you tattoo anyone when you were fourteen."

"No, sir. I was in a gang then." Spider's heart felt like it was in his throat. Like he might puke at any moment and it would just fly out of his mouth and across the room, splattering blood everywhere. "I'm not in a gang anymore."

Mr. Rivera didn't storm off. He didn't flinch, and he didn't break eye contact. "Why were you in a gang when you were fourteen?"

Spider took a measured breath and tried to focus on the facts and not the feeling of his head exploding or his heart flying across the room. "My dad died, my mom was struggling, and they were the only ones that had an internship for poor kids in the neighborhood."

"An internship?"

"Drug dealing."

"Oh."

"Sorry. Kind of a bad joke." Spider didn't look away. This was Daisy's dad. Her family. If Spider loved her, he could tell the man the truth. "I was young, so I delivered whatever they wanted me to deliver, and I kept my mouth shut." He kept his hands on the table. "In exchange, I made enough to buy groceries for my mom."

"So you were in the gang for money?"

"And protection. Luckily they discovered that I knew how to draw and they let me train with the old guy who'd been tattooing the crew since the seventies. He's the one who taught me how to tattoo."

Leonard had died of a massive heart attack when Spider was sixteen, but by then Spider was already making a name for himself.

Daisy's father cocked his head. "You must have been pretty good."

"I was the best tattoo artist in LA," Spider said. "Now I'm the best in Metlin."

Mr. Rivera smiled a little. "I appreciate a man who knows his worth."

"Oh, I'm not worth shit." Spider crossed his arms over his chest. "I tattoo people; I'm not gonna cure cancer. But I love your daughter, and she's pretty much the best person I know other than Betsy, so you can ask me whatever you want. Just don't get mad at Daisy for keeping secrets; she wanted me to meet you months ago."

"Is that right?"

"Yes, sir."

"And you didn't want to meet us?"

Spider kept his gaze steady. "I did not think that was in Daisy's best interest. I hope that makes sense."

Roberto kept his eyes steady. "Do you do drugs?"

"No. I had to smoke some weed when I was younger so I didn't stand out, but I haven't smoked or taken anything illegal for over five years."

"Do you drink?"

"Not too much." Spider's foot started tapping. "Beer's expensive, and I prefer to save money."

"For what?"

Good question. Spider had twenty-five thousand dollars sitting in a savings account. He didn't go anywhere. He didn't do anything. He didn't buy stuff. He worked and he saved his money.

For what?

"I want my own place someday," he said quietly. "My own house. My own shop. My mom had to sell the house my parents bought after my dad died and then pay rent to someone else to live in her own home." He hadn't thought about that in years. "That's messed up, right?"

Mr. Rivera nodded. "That is messed up."

"Yeah. So that's why I don't drink much. I'd rather just save the money to get my own place."

"Did you ask Daisy to stay in Metlin and not go to college?"

"Fuck no." He caught himself. "Pardon me, but no. I've been telling her for months that she needed to go, and when I asked her if she finished her forms and stuff, she always said she was working on them, and I know she was, but then she didn't fucking turn them in." Spider shook his head. "I just think it's a good idea to have a college degree, you know? If my mom'd had a degree, she wouldn't have been stuck cleaning houses after my dad died."

Mr. Rivera's eyes lit up. "Exactly. We don't know what the future is going to be like. It's better to be prepared." He spread his hands. "That's all her mother and I want."

Spider uncrossed his arms and shook his head. "If she doesn't decide to do it herself though, she's not gonna do it. She can act all easygoing, but when she gets her mind set on something—"

"It's like trying to push a bull up a hill." Mr. Rivera sighed. "My aunt is exactly the same way."

Wait. Did he and Mr. Rivera just... bond or some

shit?

"So…" Spider didn't know where to go from there. "Is Daisy okay?"

"She's with Tia Imelda. They were plotting something at the café today."

"Plotting what?"

Mr. Rivera stood. "I think you'd better come with me. I'm supposed to bring you to the café." He turned toward the door, then turned back. "I didn't tell her I'd be interrogating you before we left."

Spider stood and reached for his jacket. "She probably guessed that would happen anyway."

Mr. Rivera laughed a little. "Probably." He opened the front door and almost ran into the cheerful red wreath that Daisy had hung. "You make my daughter happy, Spider. You're a hard worker, and Bill speaks highly of you. The gang stuff? I don't care about that too much as long as you put it in the past."

Spider carefully locked up and followed Daisy's father down the stairs. "I'm trying. I really am."

———

DAISY WAS GOING TO KILL HER FATHER. HE'D sat down, listened intently when she explained the plan, and then offered to go pick up Spider when the time was right. Well, the time was right—Chino was sitting at a table in Café Maya, and Spider was not here.

Now she was stalling.

She'd pocketed the card on Spider's table days ago, but it had taken every ounce of courage she could manage to call the number. Her aunt was with her every step of the way, just like always.

Imelda handed Daisy a plate with a large piece of apple pie on it and patted her hand. "Remember, it's not personal." She glanced at the man sitting in the front of the café. "It's just business. I mean, you can *make* it personal and then keep it to business; he won't say no."

Betsy was standing with Imelda behind the counter; she handed her a fresh place setting wrapped in a paper napkin. "Make him think Spider is doing him a favor."

"And don't forget to use his mother or his grand-mother if you need to." Imelda kept her voice low. "I'll call your father if he's not here in five minutes."

Two old ladies plotting to outsmart a gang leader. Daisy couldn't have asked for better allies. "Thanks. Is Mr. Juarez coming too?"

"He and Bill are already on the way here."

Daisy walked the slice of pie over to Chino's table and set it down in front of him, taking the seat across the table. "Sorry he's not here yet. My dad is driving, and he's a slowpoke."

Chino was all smiles and good humor. "It's cool." He looked around at the tinsel tree in the corner, the holly-leaf garlands behind the register, and the frost-painted window ready to draw in Christmas customers.

"This is fucking good pie." Chino dug into his second slice.

"Tia Imelda's special." Daisy pointed to her aunt, who waved at the gangster in a dark plaid quilted shirt. "She's teaching me all the family recipes."

"She should write a book or something."

"And give away the secrets of Café Maya?" Daisy pretended to be shocked. "No, it's a Metlin institution. You know how small towns are."

Chino narrowed his eyes a little. "Yeah. So you're Spider's girl, right?"

"Yep."

"What did he want to talk to me about?" He waved back at Imelda. "Not that I don't appreciate a good piece of pie, but it's a three-hour drive."

Daisy smiled brilliantly. "We'll have to send you home with some pies for your family. Are you spending the holidays with them?"

Chino squirmed a little. "Uh, yeah. I'll go over to my mom's."

"Big family?"

The man looked confused, but he didn't hesitate to answer. "Huge family. And that's not even counting my boys."

Let's just gloss over your boys, shall we? "Me too. I mean, I only have one brother, but my mom has, like, five sisters and they all have at least three kids, so I have a million cousins, and that's not even counting my dad's cousins and their families. It's a lot."

Chino nodded thoughtfully. "And all around the area?"

"Mostly." Not even a little bit. She saw her father and Spider approaching, saw Spider stop when he realized who was in the café, and then he pushed past her father and through the door without a moment's hesitation.

"Daisy." He pulled out the chair next to her and sat down, never taking his eyes off Chino. "Hey."

"You're late." She leaned over and kissed his cheek. "Chino has been enjoying some of Imelda's apple pie."

"That reminds me, I need to tell her something real quick." He held up a finger to Chino. "Give me just one minute, will you?"

Spider rose and grabbed Daisy's hand, leading her away before Chino could question it as Roberto took a seat at one of the empty tables a few rows back.

Daisy nearly had to run to keep up. "Spider, just let me—"

"Explain." He bent down and hissed in her ear. "Very quickly, princesa. Because this is very fucked up right now."

Daisy took him by the front of his jacket and held on tight while she looked in his eyes. "Look around you right now."

Betsy was carrying the coffeepot to the front tables to offer warm-ups to Chino and Mr. Rivera. Imelda was behind the counter, and Emmie was singing out-of-tune Christmas carols with the radio in the kitchen.

The back door swung open, and Spider looked over her shoulder and frowned. "Is that—"

"Just Bill and Mr. Juarez," she said quietly. "Coming

in the back for their weekly coffee. It's a little early for it, but they decided to make an exception for today."

Spider looked around the café, his eyes going wide when he realized who all was there. "Daisy, what did you do?"

"You can't go back to Chino's crew, Spider. You joined a new one." She rose and placed a soft kiss on his mouth. "And we're not letting you go."

CHAPTER 13

"HAVE A HOLLY JOLLY CHRISTMAS" was playing on the jukebox when Spider and Daisy made it back to the table. Chino had finished his pie and was leaned back in his chair, leg kicked out into the aisle and a toothpick stuck in the corner of his mouth.

"Sorry about that." Spider slid into the seat across from him. "It's been a hectic day."

Chino glanced over his shoulder at the small crowd gathered in back. "You sure you want to talk about things here?"

Spider spread his hands and decided to go the up-front route. "Chino, man, I got nothing to hide. I'm a law-abiding citizen here." He reached over for Daisy's hand. "I don't have any secrets from my girl. That's one of the benefits to staying here. I'm a shitty liar, and I don't have to lie to anyone anymore."

Chino's eyes narrowed. "Staying here, huh?"

Spider leaned forward, and Imelda's advice burned his ears.

Keep it business.

All he cares about is money and power.

So give him money and power.

"Brother." Spider shook his head sadly. "I can't move back to the place where my mom was killed. I'd never have peace."

"I told you, you don't move back to that neighborhood. We get you a place in Boyle—"

"Why do that when I can stay here?" Spider spread his hands. "You could always tell when any of your boys was shitting you, right?"

"You know it."

"Am I shitting you now?" Spider said clearly. "I am not in that life anymore. I don't want to be. But any of your crew you send to me for ink? I promise I will treat them like my brother as long as they respect you, they respect me, and they keep it clean when they're in this town."

Chino sat back and his face was a wooden mask.

Keep it business, Spider.

"It's a lot cheaper to live here than Boyle Heights," he continued. "I can get a shop up here. I can get a house someday."

"Brother, I told you we would help with all that shit."

He reached for Daisy's hand. "My girl's whole family lives here, man. You want me to take her away from her mom? Her aunties?"

Daisy squeezed his hand, but she didn't say anything.

"See those two old guys in the back?" Spider continued quietly. "That's Bill, who runs the tattoo shop here. And Mr. Juarez, the rancher who gave me a job when I was a skinny kid who'd just lost his mom."

Chino looked over his shoulder and pressed his lips together. "I see 'em."

Daisy said, "Spider helped Mr. and Mrs. Juarez fix up their corrals a couple of months ago."

Chino looked at Daisy. "He's a real sweetheart, isn't he?"

"I think so." Daisy glanced at Mr. Juarez. "So do a lot of other people."

Spider had a sick feeling in his stomach when Betsy came over with the coffeepot. He gripped Daisy's hand, wishing she was nowhere near Chino.

Betsy asked Chino, "Can I get you a refill?"

"This is Betsy," Daisy continued, holding out her mug. "Spider lived with her and her granddaughter for a while."

"He helped me reupholster an entire couch for my bookshop," Betsy said, topping off Chino's mug. "Can you believe that? I had no idea what I was doing, but Spider knew."

The corner of Chino's mouth turned up. "He's a talented boy."

Spider glanced at Daisy, then said quietly, "Why don't you go help your aunt for a minute?"

Daisy looked at Spider, then at Chino. She nodded and left the table.

Spider waited for her to leave, then turned back to Chino. "I'm not gonna lie. I want to stay up here to make her happy. But staying up north is good business too," he said. "It's less overhead. Less exposure to... whoever you might be beefing with—I don't know, I don't want to know—and all the same benefits for your crew. You and the boys would have first priority. Hell, if you wanted to send some kids up here to train with me, I'd be cool with that too." He'd do everything in his power to get them out of the life, but he'd teach them.

Spider could tell the idea of cheap tattoos was appealing, especially if that meant that he wouldn't have to pay for Spider to set up a shop. Chino knew what rents were better than Spider did.

"And what about the next guy who takes off?" Chino asked. "If I let you out—"

"No offense, homey, but I'm not like the other guys." Spider knew when to flex and when to be humble. "Not since I was fourteen. You're not offering to set the other guys up with their own shop, are you? The other guys don't have Leonard's sketches, do they? The other guys didn't lose their moms."

Chino was silent, but Spider could tell he was considering it.

"And we both know the expensive shit is the custom work," Spider continued. "I'd still be willing to do all that. If someone in the crew wanted something done, I could come down there—"

"No." Chino's voice was hard. "If you're not in my crew, you're not in LA."

Spider was silent.

Damn, he'd been hoping to finally get to Disneyland someday.

Oh well.

"Fine," Spider said. "I'm not south of Valencia."

Chino's jaw jutted out. "If I want custom work, we meet in Vegas. You do it for free."

Spider nodded. "I'm cool with that."

"And you get any referrals from me" —Chino narrowed his eyes— "I get a... What do you call that shit?"

Spider caught on. "A finder's fee?"

"Yeah. A finder's fee." Chino looked at Spider. His eyes drifted from him to the back of the café where Daisy, Imelda, Betsy, Roberto, Bill, and Mr. Juarez had all fallen silent, waiting to see how Spider and Chino's conversation turned. "If I got a finder's fee for referrals, I'd probably be cool with that."

"Probably?"

Chino kept his voice low. "Just know that if you ever try to—"

"I won't." Spider didn't even let him finish the thought. "I been out of that life for five years, man—you think I want to change that now?"

Chino shrugged. "Some people leave, time passes, they get lazy... You know what happens."

"Is that me?" Spider leaned forward.

Chino stared at him. "No."

"For you, this is business," Spider said. "But for me it's personal." He glanced at Daisy, then looked back at Chino. "I don't want anything to happen to you, Chino. Or your boys. I mean that. You're probably one of the last people in the world who remembers my dad."

The shop where Spider's father had worked had specialized in lowriders and other classic cars that many of the older members of the gang treasured, especially Chino's father.

Chino crossed his arms over his chest. "Yeah, I remember your pops."

"I'm trying to be like my dad," Spider said. "Be that kind of man. You get me?" Spider's father was the kind of man others respected and trusted. The kind of man whose wife and kid could depend on him. The kind of man who made people safe.

And Chino's dad had been the kind of man who ran a violent crew of drug-dealing criminals.

Chino nodded a little. "I get you."

Spider offered his hand. "Respect, brother."

After what felt like an eternity, Chino took it. "Respect."

———

"WHAT DID YOU HAVE TO GIVE HIM?" DAISY PUT her head on Spider's shoulder as they sat in the driveway of her parents' house. It had been one of the longest days of her life, and it wasn't over yet. Spider was finally attending a Rivera family dinner.

"Free tattoos for life," he said. "A promise not to ever go to Southern California. And my firstborn child."

She sat up straight and her eyes went wide. "What the fuck?"

Spider laughed, then kissed her mouth. "What is that language, Daisy Rivera? I'm joking. You better not start cursing or Imelda will blame me." He looked at the lit-up house warily. "Are you sure about this? Maybe it would be better if we waited for—"

"Nope." She squeezed his hand. "You made peace with Chino, you're settling in Metlin, and we're done being secret."

"Fine." His lips pursed. "But just so you know, your dad and I agree about the school thing."

She narrowed her eyes. "I knew you two were talking before he brought you over!"

"Oh, I'm sorry. You mean when he brought me to Café Maya to be part of a plan you and your aunt plotted without even talking to me?"

Daisy wanted to feel bad about it, but it had all turned out okay in the end, so she couldn't. Much. "Betsy helped too."

He shook his head. "I should be fucking furious at

you for risking yourself that way. And risking all the rest of them."

"We didn't force anyone to be there," Daisy said. "And all those people already knew about your past. We just wanted to make sure that you and Chino both knew that your future is in Metlin."

He pulled her close and kissed her hard. "Okay, princesa. It's a damn good thing I love you so much; don't ever pull anything like that again." He opened the door of the El Camino. "Now let's go meet the family."

He was distinctly paler walking toward the house than he normally was.

Daisy took his hand. "You survived a meeting with your old boss this morning, but a bunch of little kids and aunties are scaring you?"

"Chino's world I understand." He shook his head. "This one I haven't been part of for nearly ten years."

"What world is that?"

"Normal-people world."

Daisy shook her head, making sure her face was extra sad. "Spider, I hate to break it to you" —she pushed open the door to the raucous sound of women laughing in the kitchen, half a dozen teenagers blasting music in the living room, and a clutch of men shouting at the television as a Nerf bullet sailed past them and into the night— "but my family is not even close to normal."

Spider nodded. "Cool. I might be able to blend in."

———

HE DIDN'T, OF COURSE. NOT YET. BUT WHILE Daisy was dragged into the kitchen to be interrogated by the aunties, Kiko shook her boyfriend's hand and silently promised in the language of siblings to take care of the new guy. Daisy raised her eyebrows menacingly. Kiko shrugged like she had nothing to worry about.

A hundred questions and three large pans of enchiladas later, they were finally sitting down to dinner, old people and teenagers at one table, parents and young adults at another, and the last of the little ones running in between, dropping crumbs everywhere.

Spider sat next to Daisy, silently clutching her hand under the table.

"So Spider, how long have you worked at Bill and Ruby's place?" Daisy's aunt started.

"About ten months," he said quietly. "So far it's good."

The table had fallen silent while he answered. Her family had quickly learned that if you wanted an answer from Spider, you had to listen closely.

"And what do you think about Daisy not going away to school?" Daisy's mom dropped that bomb while she was serving Kiko enchiladas.

The melted, stringy cheese hung in the air, like all Daisy's plans for the future.

Her dad quietly said, "Alicia..."

"What? He's her boyfriend now; I think it's important to know his opinion."

Daisy turned to Spider. "You don't have to—"

"I think degrees are good to have," Spider said. "And Daisy is smart enough to go wherever she wants." He glanced at her and raised an eyebrow. "But I also know that if you're not really into what you're studying, it's pretty useless, right?" He shrugged. "I mean, that was my experience in school. Not that I finished."

She saw a flash of panic in his eyes, as if he'd said something wrong.

"Now that you're staying in Metlin," Daisy said casually, "you can study for your GED if you want."

He squeezed her hand again. "Yeah, that's a good idea."

Alicia pursed her lips. "I like him."

Tia Imelda shouted from the other table, "I told you!"

"Hey Mom," Kiko said casually.

"What do you need, mijo?" Alicia preemptively reached for the spatula to serve more enchiladas. "How many do you want?"

"I have enough enchiladas." He cleared his throat, trying to repress a smile. "So my guidance counselor was telling me that because my grades and extracurriculars were so good last year, I should try for early admission a couple of places for next year. That way if I get in, I can work on what I'd need for financial aid and all that."

Alicia was nodding and serving more enchiladas. "That's a good idea."

Roberto frowned. "I thought you wanted to do the business program at Fresno State."

"That's still an option," Kiko said. "But Ms. Sousa also suggested I apply to Stanford, so I did that, and I just got a letter that I was accepted."

The big table fell so silent even the little kids stopped running around in circles.

Alicia's arm was frozen in midserve. "You what?"

Daisy's mouth fell open. "You got into Stanford?"

Spider nodded. "That's cool, man."

Alicia sprang to her feet, dropping the spatula as she let out an ear-piercing scream. "Roberto, our baby got into Stanford!"

Her father's eyes were getting teary when he rose and walked over to Kiko, his arms were spread wide. "Guess you're not going into the construction business after all."

"That's okay, right?"

"How could you even ask that?" Roberto openly wiped away tears as he embraced his son.

And as the table erupted in excited shouts and a million questions, Daisy leaned back and caught Kiko's eye over her father's shoulder. Her little brother winked at her.

"Sneaky little punk," Daisy muttered. "I owe him one now."

Spider put his arm around her. "Why didn't you apply to Stanford?"

She shrugged. "They tried. Mom and Dad begged me. My aunts and uncles all called me. Mr. Talbot nearly wept when I told him I was staying local."

Spider cocked his head. "Why not?"

She turned to look at him. "I know what I want. I always have."

"I still think you should get the degree." Spider hugged her shoulders. "But it's your decision."

"You're supposed to be on my side," she said, laying her head in the curve of his shoulder.

"I am." Spider kissed her forehead. "Always."

"And forever." She looked at him from the corner of her eye.

"Yeah." Spider's smile was slow and sweet. "Forever, princesa."

———

The end?

EPILOGUE

Fifteen years later…

SPIDER WAITED at the foot of the staircase, running his hand along the old banister that smelled of lemon oil and beeswax.

"Do you need help?" He glanced up the stairs.

"No!"

They'd spent two weeks cleaning their small house from top to bottom, polishing the restored woodwork, cleaning up the garden and filling containers with spring blooms.

Daisy's parents had offered to host the graduation party at their house, but his wife had insisted on holding the party in their small home. Spider did insist on letting Daisy's aunt Dolores cater the party though. Daisy had been killing herself with graduation requirements that semester, all while juggling a satellite branch of Café Maya she'd recently opened on the campus where she was graduating. The last thing she needed to do on her own college graduation day was cook for seventy people.

"Okay." She stepped onto the landing and looked down. "I look ridiculous."

Spider grinned. "You look fucking hot."

"Hot?" She tried to smother the smile, but she couldn't. "These hats? They're clearly not meant for people with curly hair."

He couldn't stop smiling as she walked down the steps toward him.

The cap did smash down her spiraled curls a little, but her black robe was immaculately ironed and the gold ropes hanging from her neck fell down and framed her boobs nicely.

"I like it." He picked up a gold tassel. "My baby got the smart ropes."

She raised one eyebrow. "They're called honor cords, and I have plans for them later when my family is gone."

He narrowed his eyes. "Princesa, don't give me a hard-on when we're supposed to be picking up your aunt in fifteen minutes."

Tia Imelda had insisted on driving with Spider; she was getting older and was convinced that her nephew drove too fast on the highway. She told Roberto that Spider drove more carefully.

Really, Spider knew Imelda just liked riding in the silver 1963 Buick Riviera he and Daisy had bought and fixed up three years before. It was Daisy's present to him for their ten-year anniversary and only proved that his wife was fucking awesome.

"Oh!" Daisy started up the stairs. "I have an idea for my cap." She paused and turned around. "Do we have time?"

He checked his watch. "Five minutes and we need to go pick up your aunt. I'm not showing up late for my wife's college graduation. She'll kill me."

Daisy rolled her eyes. "Ha ha. Five minutes should be enough. And if you drove faster—"

"Getting stopped by some asshole cop on the way to my wife's graduation is also not in the plan." Which was inevitable if he went over the speed limit. He might be a business owner, celebrated graphic artist, and upstanding citizen these days, but he still had a fucking spider tattooed on his head and a neck that said "gang-banger" to law enforcement.

Spider tapped his watch. "Five minutes. I'll start the car."

She glanced toward the kitchen. "Do you think Dolores—?"

"Daisy!"

"Spider." She put her hands on her hips. "What? It's a big party."

And his girl was a perfectionist. It was what made her such a great baker, amazing businesswoman, and honor student.

Spider took a deep breath. "Everything is going to be

fine. Your family is going to have everything perfect because they are you and you are them." He walked up the stairs and kissed her forehead. "Now, will you go fix your hair thing please so we aren't late for your graduation ceremony?"

"Fine." Her cheeks were a little pink. "You look pretty hot in a suit."

"Yeah?"

She twirled her smart ropes. "Plans for you later, remember?"

And there his dick went. "Evil." He lifted a finger and shook it in her face. "You're fucking evil, princesa."

She laughed and escaped to the upstairs bathroom. She knew exactly what she did to him.

Minx.

Spider grabbed his sunglasses, keys, and went out to the car to see Imelda already in the front yard, leaning against the Buick and wearing a formfitting blue dress, a bright yellow scarf, and a pair of giant sunglasses that made her look like a movie star.

Spider let out a long whistle. "Looks like I'm driving the two most beautiful women in Metlin today." He glanced at her walker. "Did you walk all the way here?"

"It's only two blocks," she said. "It's good for me."

"How long did it take you?"

She grimaced. "Too damn long. And if you tell Roberto I'm swearing now, I'll poison you with a cookie."

Spider didn't try to hide the smile. "I won't breathe a word."

Imelda stood straight with the help of her walker and shifted to the side so Spider could open the door for her. "You're a smart boy, Manuel."

"I know I am." He opened the door and made sure she was situated before he folded her walker. Tia Imelda was the only one in the family who insisted on calling him by his given name, and Spider was okay with it. It was probably good that someone remembered what it was.

"Are Emmie and her young man coming to the graduation?"

"No, not enough tickets," Spider said. "But they'll be at the party later."

"Good. I need to meet this one. He looks like he might stick."

Spider smiled. "Yeah. I think he might."

Betsy had passed a few years before, leaving a giant hold in Spider's life and making Emmie the reluctant owner of Metlin Books.

He missed Betsy. Though the old woman had lived a good long life, it didn't feel like it was enough. But as she had once told him: you can never have enough time with family.

Spider was just glad Emmie had returned to Metlin after living in San Francisco for so many years. He couldn't lie; spending time anywhere near the city still made him nervous.

He worked freely in Las Vegas, as he and Chino had agreed to many years before, but he never violated his pact with his old boss and headed into LA even though Chino had been killed seven years before.

Spider didn't worry about his safety anymore. Not really. His work had been featured in trade magazines, and he counted some pretty fucking famous people among his clients. When anyone asked who the best tattoo artist on the West Coast was, his name was in the top five.

It was enough to satisfy his ego and still maintain his privacy.

Daisy came running out of the house, her hand holding her hat on her head and her black robes flying behind her.

"I'm here! I'm done." She jumped in the car and grinned at Imelda. "Did you walk down here?"

"Don't ask me how long it took." She reached over from the back seat and put a gnarled hand on Daisy's shoulder. "You look beautiful, mi hija."

"Thank you, Tia."

As Spider backed out of the driveway and headed down the street, his wife and her aunt kept talking.

"So you have everything you want now, yes? A bakery—"

"Two bakeries," Spider corrected.

"—a beautiful house," Imelda continued, "a handsome husband. And now a college degree."

Spider was skeptical about the handsome part, but he was fucking grateful that Daisy finally had her degree.

"It took me long enough, right? Maybe Dad will finally stop pestering me."

"There's always grad school," Spider said.

"Bite your tongue." She reached over and playfully hit his arm as Spider grinned.

It had taken her a long time, but the five years she'd been working on it had been filled with challenges, joy, disappointments, and triumphs.

It had been filled with life. And life didn't always take a straight path.

He stretched his arm across the back of the bench seat and watched Daisy pin the black cap to her hair as they drove.

She was the light of his life. The best fucking thing that had ever been given to him. If she said she wanted the moon, Spider would figure out a way to steal it.

Then again, Daisy never asked for much.

So he could only give her everything.

To read more Love Stories on 7th and Main,
look for Emmie's story, INK, at all major retailers.

NOW AVAILABLE: INK

EMMIE ELLIOT LASTED three breaths in the old book-shop, her measured exhalations stirring dust motes that danced in the afternoon light streaming in from the large display windows that looked over Main Street. She backed out the front door and turned her back on Metlin Books, staring at the lazy midday traffic driving south on 7th Avenue. Then she bent over, braced her hands on her knees, and let her auburn hair fall, shielding her face from the afternoon sun.

Daisy walked out of the corner shop and came to stand beside her. "What's going on? You're even paler than usual."

"I can't do it."

"Can't do what?"

Emmie straightened. "I can't sell the shop."

Daisy's eyes went wide. "I thought you and your gran—"

"Yeah." Emmie took a deep breath, clearing the dust from her lungs. "I know."

What are you doing, Emmie?

She had no idea.

She'd spent her whole life trying to get away from this town. The bookstore was her grandmother's. Sure, she'd grown up in it, and sure, she worked in a bookstore in San Francisco, but that was just temporary. She was just doing that until something happened. Something bigger. More important. More... something.

Emmie was twenty-seven and still waiting for something big to happen. She had a job she tolerated, an apartment she loved. No husband, no boyfriend, a mother she barely spoke to. She didn't even have a cat.

Her assets in the world consisted of a newish car, a very small inheritance from her Grandma Betsy, a circle of carefully chosen friends, and a three-unit retail building on the corner of Main Street and 7th Avenue, right in the heart of Metlin, a sleepy town in the middle of Central California.

She and her grandmother had talked about it a year ago, when they knew the cancer wasn't going into remission. Emmie was supposed to sell the building and use the proceeds as a nest egg for...

They'd never really talked about that part.

"What's going on, Em? What are you thinking?" Daisy frowned and twisted a lock of dark wavy hair back in the bun on top of her head. It was afternoon, but she was still wearing her apron from baking that morning. With her tan skin, dark eyes, and retro apron, Daisy looked like an updated Latina June Cleaver if you didn't notice the tattoos at her wrists.

Her friend Tayla had offered to accompany her from San Francisco, but Emmie had refused. Emmie was taking a full two weeks off work from Bay City Books, but Tayla worked at a big accounting firm and couldn't afford to take the time off. She'd never been to Metlin and had no desire to visit. Tayla was a city girl to her bones.

It's fine, Emmie had told her. *It's not like I have any reason to stay. My mom cleaned out my grandma's apartment. I'll visit Daisy and Spider, sign papers to put the place on the market, and leave.*

Emmie straightened her button-down blouse and played with the buttons on the sleeve of her cardigan. She wasn't dressed for Metlin; she was dressed for an upscale bookshop in Union Square. If anyone from her childhood were to pass by, they would have a hard time putting Emmie's sleek hair and tidy, professional appearance together with the rumpled girl who'd spent most of her life hiding behind a book.

She didn't belong in Metlin anymore. She never had. She'd always wanted a bigger life. A more important life around people who liked music and art and travel, not farmers and mechanics and ranchers.

Daisy said, "I know you must have sentimental

attachment to the building, but I'm not sure you realize—"

"How bad it was?" Emmie picked at a thread on one of her buttons, twisting it between her thumb and forefinger. "I know how bad it was. Grandma was completely up-front with me."

Emmie had no illusions about the state of Metlin Books. The shop was barely hanging on. The only thing her grandma'd had going for her was that she owned the building, the apartment above it, and rented to two successful neighbors, a family hardware business and Café Maya, Daisy's restaurant.

She walked over and sat on the cast-iron bench in front of the bookstore windows, kicking at the doggie water dish chained to the bench. The dish that had remained dry since her grandmother had passed six months before. "Bookstores are not a good bet."

"Not generally, no."

"She told me not to be noble." Emmie eyed the water dish again. Then she took the water bottle out of her purse and dumped the contents in the bowl. "We had a plan. Sell the shop with provisions for you and Ethan—"

"Leave me and Ethan out of it," Daisy said. "I loved your grandma, but I think I can speak for Ethan—"

"Speak for me how?" Ethan Vasquez, owner of Main Street Hardware, set down the A-frame sign advertising daily deals and walked toward Daisy and Emmie. "Em, you all right?"

Daisy kept talking. "We both loved Betsy, but this is your life and inheritance, so don't worry about us."

"What's going on?" Ethan and Daisy hovered over her.

Daisy straightened. "Emmie's not sure about selling the shop."

"Great!"

"No," Daisy said. "Not great. This was not the plan."

And all of Emmie's friends knew how much Emmie liked a plan. She was famous for them. Emmie would plan a night out three days in advance and email a detailed schedule to everyone "so they were on the same page." She didn't do spontaneous. The idea of returning to Metlin permanently was giving her heart palpitations.

You're waiting, a little voice in her head whispered. *What are you waiting for?*

Ethan crossed his arms over his barrel chest and let out a long breath. "You know I can't be unbiased on this one."

"So stay out of it."

"I *am* staying out of it." He scratched his beard thoughtfully. "That's why I'm reminding her I can't be unbiased."

Emmie looked up and took a deep breath. "Don't be unbiased. I want your opinion."

"A new owner is likely to kick me and Dad out," he said. "Just when I'm turning things around. You know that. Our shop is huge, and space on Main Street is at a premium these days. A new owner would likely split our store in half and make double what we're paying now. So of course I want you to stay." He crouched down. "Metlin's different, Emmie. It's not the same town you left."

"That I can agree with," Daisy said.

"And I know the store needs work," Ethan continued, "but me and my dad would help you out. Anything you need. We're free labor after all the favors Betsy did for us over the years. You know that, right?"

Ethan's big brown eyes pleaded with her. Emmie looked past him to the new paint on his store, the fresh awning, the racks of vegetable starts for backyard gardens. Main Street Hardware had been flailing until Ethan came back from college four years ago and revamped his family business.

Now, instead of depending on the dwindling business of the retirement crowd, Main Street Hardware appealed to young do-it-yourselfers in their late twenties like Ethan and his buddies who were buying the old Craftsman cottages south of downtown and fixing them up. Ethan led workshops on container gardening, and his dad taught plasterwork and hardwood-floor-refinishing courses.

Beyond the hardware store, Café Maya bustled with midday customers. It was a narrow café and bakery started by Daisy's grandmother Maya, who'd come from Oaxaca and started the restaurant with determination and a treasure trove of recipes. Daisy's mother had modernized the menu, and Daisy had added a bakery. Café Maya was a Metlin institution and business had remained solid.

Beyond Emmie's building, stretching west, sat the rest of downtown. Sitting at the base of the Sierra Nevada mountains, Metlin had never been big enough to attract attention from any of the big chains. It had only ever had one bookstore, Metlin Books. And for as long as anyone could remember, it had been run by the Elliot family. Emmie's great-grandfather had bought the building and started a book and toy store. Eventually the toys left and her grandmother had focused on the books. Emmie's mom, despite her bookish roots, had never been a reader and lived an itinerant life as a working musician. She was happy, but Metlin wasn't her home.

But for Emmie—growing up in the fishbowl of Metlin—the bookshop had been her home, her refuge, and the gateway to a much larger world.

"I have an apartment in San Francisco," she said quietly. "Friends. A life. A job."

Ethan asked, "Aren't you working in a bookstore up there?"

"Yeah."

He frowned. "But you *own* a bookstore here. Why on earth would you live in San Francisco, pay God knows what in rent, and get paid to work at someone else's business when you could own your own business here doing exactly the same thing?"

Daisy said, "Back off."

"She knows I'm right." He stood and pointed at Emmie. "You know I'm right."

Emmie's stayed silent. She didn't deal with confrontation well, but Ethan wasn't entirely wrong. How many times had she tried to change something at the bookstore she worked at in the city, only to be told "that wasn't the way things were done" at Bay City Books?

Still, she hesitated. "I manage a store. I don't know if I could run a business. My grandma wasn't like your dad. She didn't give me a lot of responsibility in the shop. I know nothing about bookkeeping or—"

"You'd figure it out," he said. "You're one of the smartest people I know. You helped me with my place when I was drowning."

She shrugged. "You would have come up with those ideas on your own with enough time."

"I doubt it. You have a great brain for marketing. You know what people like now. How to put everything online. How to find the right customers."

Daisy shook her head. "Books are a tough business, Ethan. I know exactly how much Betsy was making with this place, and rent from your place and my café was the only thing paying her bills. Competing with online retailers—"

"Can't be any tougher than competing with the megamart hardware stores," Ethan said. "Emmie knows—"

"Emmie knows"—Emmie stood and cut them both off—"she needs to spend some time thinking about this."

Daisy's mouth fought off a smile. "Emmie also knows she needs to stop talking in third person, right? Because it's obnoxious."

"Whatever you do," Ethan said, "don't talk to Asshole Adrian until you've made up your mind."

Emmie frowned. "Adrian? Adrian from high school?"

"Yeah, Adrian Saroyan. He's in real estate now. And he's an asshole."

Daisy tried to shove Ethan away. "Ignore him. You know he never liked Adrian."

"Nobody likes Adrian." Ethan let Daisy shove him. "You were the only one who liked him, Em."

"Me and the female half of my high school class." Emmie watched Daisy—a foot shorter than Ethan—shove the big man back to his shop.

Ethan repositioned his sign. "He's a dipshit and an asshole."

Daisy said, "He stole your girlfriend; that's the only reason you hate him."

"That's not the only reason," Ethan muttered. "Just one of them."

Emmie left them bickering and walked back into the bookshop. She stood in the mosaic-tiled entryway and examined it with critical eyes.

Pros: She owned it, free and clear. It had a recognizable name and a good location. It was a beautiful space with huge built-in shelves and custom woodwork her giant bookstore in San Francisco tried to imitate but never really could. Metlin Books had history. Charm. And a two-bedroom apartment over the shop. If she lived here, she would have no commute and no rent.

Cons: Profits under her grandmother had been pretty much zero. The only real income was from renting the rest of the building, and that just paid the bills. The bookshop was a ton of work with a very small profit margin. She'd be solely responsible for it. There would be no vacation days accrued. No retirement plan. No one else paying the bills. No one to call in sick to.

But it's mine.

Yes, it was. Emmie walked around the shop, rifling through the stacks of used books her grandmother had collected. Most of the new inventory was so old she could never sell it at cover price. She'd be starting over.

Betsy had stocked lots of romances, but nothing modern. There was a nice stack of vintage Harlequins she might be able to sell online to a collector. She needed far more new names. Romance ran bookstores. She'd have to get an updated selection and figure out how to buy from self-published authors who made up so many of the new writers these days. It was something she'd pushed for at Bay City, but the owners were complete snobs about self-publishing.

The shop had a good mystery section, but it leaned

toward cozies. Her grandmother hadn't cared for thrillers or any dark psychology.

Hardly any literary fiction or poetry, but in Metlin that was probably a safe call.

Nonfiction was in dire need of updating. Judging from the traffic at Ethan's store, gardening manuals and idea books would probably sell well, as would interior design and home-improvement stuff.

With growing tourist traffic from the national park, local history and outdoor guides could be a winner.

Emmie wandered across the shop and looked out the windows just as a trio of motorcycles revved their engines at the intersection of 7th and Main. Emmie watched two guys in an animated discussion in front of the custom-car-upholstery shop and listened to the buzz of music and voices from Ice House Brews that sat catty-corner to Metlin Books at the intersection. Directly across from her on Main was Bombshell Tattoos. Beyond it, a specialty cigar and smoking club. A couple with vividly dyed hair and heavy ink left the tattoo shop hand in hand and walked past the T-shirt shop on Main headed toward Top Shelf Comics and Games.

What books would that couple read? How about the guys in front of the car shop? Graphic novels? Steam-punk? Auto history?

Emmie watched from behind her windows as a trio of women dragged a giant mirror from one of the antique shops farther down 7th, laughing as they tried to fit it in the back of a battered pickup truck. Decorating books. DIY manuals.

Across the street, a graffiti-style mural decorated the front of an art-supply store next to an auto-body shop. Art history books? Political science?

Ethan was right. Metlin was changing. The industrial and the traditional were colliding and creating something odd and new and more than a little cool. And Emmie realized the bookshop—her bookshop—was sitting right in the middle of it all.

Maybe she hadn't belonged in the old Metlin, but times changed. Towns changed. People changed.

This was not in the plan, her logical side said.

Maybe the plan needs to change.

Emmie pulled out her phone. Her finger shook as she touched Tayla's number and waited for her best friend to pick up.

"Hey!" she answered. "Did you get everything signed? How's Daisy?"

Emmie took a deep breath, stirring the dust again. "I have an idea. And it might be crazy or it might be amazing."

"If it's a really good idea, it'll be both. And it might also involve handcuffs or Silly String."

She blinked. "Silly String?"

"Do you really want to know? You sound weird."

"I didn't sign any papers to sell the shop."

"Okay…?"

"I think you should quit your job, move down to Metlin with me, and help me reopen the bookshop."

Tayla didn't say a word.

Emmie squeezed her eyes shut. "I know it sounds nuts, but you can have free rent."

Her best friend remained silent.

"Tayla, please say something."

"Maybe it's because I caught one of the senior partners staring at my boobs *again* today, but I am actually considering this."

Emmie tried not to jump up and down with excitement.

"That's not a yes. Or a no," Tayla said. "But… maybe?"

"I'll take maybe."

"Tell you what, it's Friday. I'll catch the train tomorrow morning," Tayla said. "I can't guarantee anything, but I want to see this hick town you claim to hate but now suddenly want me to move to."

"I'll meet you at the station."

"Is this a result of valley fever?" Tayla asked. "I've read about that, you know."

"I don't have valley fever."

"Isn't that something someone with valley fever would say?"

Emmie squeezed her eyes shut. "Tayla, I can't explain it. I just think it might be awesome. Or nuts. But you know how you were getting on my case last month for always being cautious and never taking chances?"

"Yep."

"This…" Emmie turned around in the empty shop. "This is a chance."

———

Modern romance, small town charm.
Love Stories on 7th and Main are now available at all major retailers in ebook, audiobook, and paperback.
INK - HOOKED - GRIT

ABOUT THE AUTHOR

ELIZABETH HUNTER is a seven-time *USA Today* and international best-selling author of romance, contemporary fantasy, and paranormal mystery. Based in Central California, she travels extensively to write fantasy fiction exploring world mythologies, history, and the universal bonds of love, friendship, and family. She has published over forty works of fiction and sold over a million books worldwide. She is the author of the Glimmer Lake series, Love Stories on 7th and Main, the Elemental Legacy series, the Irin Chronicles, the Cambio Springs Mysteries, and other works of fiction.

ALSO BY ELIZABETH HUNTER

Contemporary Romance

The Genius and the Muse

7th and Main

Ink

Hooked

Grit

Sweet

Glimmer Lake

Suddenly Psychic

Semi-Psychic Life

Psychic Dreams

Moonstone Cove

Runaway Fate

Fate Actually

Fate Interrupted

The Elemental Mysteries

A Hidden Fire

This Same Earth

The Force of Wind

A Fall of Water

The Stars Afire

The Elemental World

Building From Ashes

Waterlocked

Blood and Sand

The Bronze Blade

The Scarlet Deep

A Very Proper Monster

A Stone-Kissed Sea

Valley of the Shadow

The Elemental Legacy

Shadows and Gold

Imitation and Alchemy

Omens and Artifacts

Obsidian's Edge (anthology)

Midnight Labyrinth

Blood Apprentice

The Devil and the Dancer

Night's Reckoning

Dawn Caravan

The Bone Scroll

The Elemental Covenant

Saint's Passage

Martyr's Promise

Paladin's Kiss

(Spring/Summer 2022)

The Irin Chronicles

The Scribe

The Singer

The Secret

The Staff and the Blade

The Silent

The Storm

The Seeker

The Cambio Springs Series

Long Ride Home

Shifting Dreams

Five Mornings

Desert Bound

Waking Hearts

Linx & Bogie Mysteries

A Ghost in the Glamour

A Bogie in the Boat

Made in the USA
Las Vegas, NV
10 December 2023